Lords of Trillium

THE NIGHTSHADE CHRONICLES

BOOK I
Nightshade City

BOOK II
The White Assassin

BOOK III
Lords of Trillium

Lords of Trillium

HILARY WAGNER

Holiday House / New York

Library of Congress Cataloging-in-Publication Data

Wagner, Hilary.
Lords of Trillium / by Hilary Wagner. — First edition.
pages cm. — (Nightshade chronicles ; book 3)
Summary: "The conclusion to the Nightshade Chronicles reveals
the secret of the Nightshade rats' unique powers and
resolves old rivalries and conflicts"— Provided by publisher.
ISBN 978-0-8234-2413-9 (hardcover)
[1. Fantasy. 2. Rats—Fiction.] I. Title.
PZ7.W12417Lo 2014
[Fic]—dc23
2013031299

For Eric, Vincent, and Nomi,
my three favorite rats

Contents

Lords of Trillium

Acknowledgments

MANY THANKS to my husband, Eric. His patience and support never cease to amaze me. He puts up with the endless stream of chaos and deadlines . . . and me. If that's not true love, I don't know what is. Everything's so much sweeter with your best friend and love of your life in your corner.

Thanks so much to my brilliant editor, Julie Amper, and everyone at Holiday House who played a part in the Lords of Trillium, including John Briggs, Mary Cash, Terry Borzumato-Greenberg, and the wonderfully detailed copy editor, George Newman. I'm indebted to Holiday House for taking a chance on an unknown author and her first book, *Nightshade City*. Their belief in this series has been unwavering and inspiring. It has been my privilege to be part of the Holiday House family.

Thank you to Genevieve Ching, who sent me an article on a volcano in Papua New Guinea, which I held onto for over a year, knowing it would lead to inspiration for this book.

Marietta Zacker, my agent at Nancy Gallt, deserves loads of

hugs and a massive thank you. She is a trusted advisor, friend, and a true passionista. I'd be lost in this crazy world of publishing without her. Thank you, Marietta, for all you do.

Last but not least, thank you, Craig...for everything. I hope I did you proud.

CHAPTER ONE
Hallowtide

As the sky darkened, Juniper and Vincent tightened their grip on the bus's undercarriage. It lurched forward, rolling into downtown Trillium. Juniper, eager to be free of the heavy fumes, inhaled a long breath as the bus picked up speed. Of late, teams of rats had gone missing. Several Hunter rats who'd set out to find food for the growing city had not returned. At first everyone blamed it on chance. Perhaps the team of Hunters got caught in a trap, run over as they slipped across a street, electrocuted by a live wire—after all, hazards Topside were endless—but when two more teams of rats vanished, Juniper and the Council knew that there was nothing random about the disappearances. The Nightshade rats were being targeted.

Juniper could not imagine anyone who might harbor hatred for his citizens. He thought of Killdeer, but he and his regime were long gone. There were the dock rats, but they never cared about others' comings and goings unless it interfered with their profitable theft of food from the many cargo ships that docked on the shores of Hellgate Sea. Moreover, his Hunters were well trained. They knew to stay far away from the toughened dock rats, a hard-bitten crew with little pity for any creature, rat or otherwise. There were a few rats who chose to dwell in Trillium, but what would be their gain? Dogs rarely bothered them, and cats mostly steered clear, knowing full well that their chances against a sturdy Trillium rat were slim to none. So who, then? He could only surmise the Topsiders were behind it, but why? Since the dawn of the Catacombs, rats had had little need to live Topside, and those who did stayed hidden or dwelled in places where most self-respecting humans rarely traveled.

He looked over at Vincent. The wind picked up, ruffling his black fur. Fall had swept in quickly, a damp, unforgiving cold. Nightshade City's food supply was stocked for the moment, but that would change quickly if the number of Hunters kept dwindling. Rats in Nightshade could come and go as they pleased. Juniper didn't want to ban that, but if any more rats went missing, he'd be forced to.

The bus idled at its next stop. Juniper and Vincent dropped to the asphalt. Under a leaden cloud of exhaust, they dashed from behind a tire and vanished into the alley behind the Brimstone Building, which sat in the center of Trillium City. They would search every alley if need be to find the lost citizens. As members of the Council, they had taken an oath. It was their sworn duty.

Hastening around the corner, they slid under a Dumpster, watching for enemies. "Topher's group always starts their hunt here," whispered Vincent. "They spread out through the city in teams." Cautiously, he stepped out from under the Dumpster and surveyed their surroundings: nothing but rubbish and gray puddles—not even the slightest scent of rat.

Sitting down, Juniper opened his tattered rucksack. It had been with him since before Killdeer took over the Catacombs. Maddy had made it for him all those years ago. He retrieved a thin silver tag. He felt the clean edges of the metal disk, the number 111 etched on its face. It was his brother's tag from his time in the lab. He wondered about him often, hoping Billycan had stayed . . . good. They'd given him the cure for the horrible, mind-altering drugs forced upon him in the Topsiders' lab, but still Juniper had doubts. What if its effects were fleeting? Cures sometimes wore off. But no matter what the truth was, Juniper wished his brother were with him now. If any rat could sniff out the lost Hunters it would be Billycan. Admittedly he'd been cruel and merciless, but he *had* commanded an army for over a decade and was a masterful tactician, expert in tracking and pursuit. If anyone could find the Hunters it would be Billycan . . . if only Juniper could find *him.*

"Do you really think he could help us locate them?" asked Vincent as Juniper put the tag back into his satchel.

Heavy footsteps sounded above their heads. Whatever was lurking on top of the Dumpster was far larger than any cat. They readied their claws.

Vincent's nose twitched. *A raccoon,* he mouthed.

As if the creature had heard him, a rangy raccoon screeched and wailed, hissing down at them from his Dumpster perch. He had several questionable-looking apples in his thick black paws, holding them protectively against his chest.

"We don't want trouble," said Juniper evenly. "We're looking for some friends, who've gone missing, I'm afraid."

Juniper might not have wanted trouble, but the raccoon

seemed to be of a different mind-set. Raccoons were highly territorial and could be irrational. The disheveled raccoon raged at them, screaming on in a jumbled language rats likened to gibberish. He pulled his arm back, launching one of his rotten apples at them.

Vincent and Juniper fled in opposite directions. The apple slammed into the wall behind Vincent, bursting into a slimy green pulp on the bricks and spattering runny chunks all over him.

Wiping his face, Vincent growled angrily. He headed straight for the Dumpster, the raccoon's bravado fading as he caught Vincent's infuriated expression. Muttering, Vincent picked up a sizable rock. "I hate raccoons."

He ran.

Lungs burning, he stole through the musty corridors—a mad fiend. He hid his ghastly goods in corners, near doorways, nailing them to walls, even stringing them up from the ceilings. He slapped his tail against the dirt wall, delighted with the sheer wickedness of it all, eager to give each and every resident the fright they deserved . . . for it was *that* time again. With a cunning grin, he glanced down a corridor. It was late. Most had turned in for the night. All the better, he thought. It was no fun working someone into a lather in the middle of the day, now was it?

He laughed softly. Never in his wildest dreams did he think he'd be here, in this moment, in *this* place! Something had driven him to come here, though, an urge he could not explain. As instinctively as birds migrate south for winter or spiders spin their intricate webs, he'd landed here as if he'd known the way all along. Though he'd arrived only a year ago, he was already in command. Once again the masses seemed to gravitate to him. He marveled at his influence. What made so many follow *him*, of all rats?

He snorted. After all that had transpired, he'd been looking for a life of solitude, but here he was running a kingdom. Once, he'd relished his power, but now . . .

Someone was coming! As the footsteps drew closer, he ducked into a corner, making sure his snaky tail and long feet were hidden from view. Oh, this was going to be good. He was really going to petrify this rat, whoever the unlucky soul was. He sniffed the air. It was a male. Billycan grinned, barely able to keep still, a fire burning inside him that he hadn't felt in some time. The sheer terror might just kill the poor fellow.

"It's hard to imagine the Topsiders ever thought highly of us," said Clover, standing over an open journal. "It seems they've *always* hated us, trying to eradicate us with their traps and poisons. I mean, we moved underground in the first place to get away from *them*."

Last year Oleander and Carn, later joined by Clover, Vincent, and the rest of the young Council members, had begun retrieving all the journals and letters from the swamp. The books and papers had been left by the Trillium scientists who had lived there. Members of Dresden's colony of bats had been helping transport the journals back to Nightshade. Clover and Vincent pored over them, enthralled.

Vincent scratched behind his ear, finding a small piece of apple skin he'd missed while cleaning himself after his earlier altercation with the raccoon. "Well, Juniper seems to think they're not all so bad. I remember . . . the little boy in the brownstone. That night changed our lives. Without his help, I don't know how things would have turned out."

"True," said Clover, "but I wonder how he feels about us now . . . four years older."

Vincent smiled. "Well . . . it's been four years for me as well, and I still think *he's* all right."

"When I read some of these entries about the founders of Trillium City, it's hard to believe humans could be anything *but* cruel." Clover walked over to another journal and glowered at the open pages. "Did you read this one?" She pointed an accusing claw at the entry. "It says here Trillium's founders legalized something called 'ratting.' They used us for sport at their public houses—setting us loose in makeshift fighting rings so dogs could tear us apart! The dog who killed the most of us was proclaimed the winner—lining his master's pockets in the process."

"Yes, it's all very upsetting," said Vincent, "but . . . did you read the *entire* journal?" He gave her a shrewd grin.

"Well, no . . . not yet," Clover replied.

Vincent flipped through the journal to one of the very last pages. He pointed to the center paragraph. "Read."

Clover eyed the page skeptically. Suddenly she leaned in close. She read the last few sentences out loud. "'A small group of angry citizens protested outside City Hall for days, claiming the sport to be inhumane not only to the rats, but the dogs as well, owing to the fact that on frequent occasions Trillium rats would collectively go after a dog, maiming it before a single rat could be harmed. Once again, Trillium rats have proved that they are not only strong, but clever. Rather than scatter and risk dying separately, united they were able to defeat the dog.'" She looked up at Vincent. "Some of the Topsiders actually *tried* to stop these fights, thinking them unjust?"

Vincent nodded. "It wasn't only the scientists who moved to the swamp who were on our side. Some Topsiders thought *all* creatures should have the same right to live that humans do."

"Do you think any Topsiders still feel that way?"

"Well, those Topsiders—the ones who broke into the lab and freed Billycan and the others—they seemed to feel we were worth something . . . and that wasn't all that long ago." He stared vacantly at the heavy door that led back to the Catacombs. "Animal rights activists, that's what they're called. I read some of them won't even eat meat. Can you imagine that? So I guess there are some who still feel it's not right to kill living creatures of any kind—even rats."

"Do you think the Topsiders—the humans—are the ones targeting us?"

"I'm not sure. What if there's some unseen enemy out there, someone who hates us even more than humans?" Vincent thought about who could hate them so much. He glanced down at his leg, never the same since that night in the Catacombs when Billycan freed him from the heavy silver chalice, Killdeer's former throne, that had fallen on him. After his broken bone finally healed he was left with a slight limp, and when the weather was foul, which was often in Trillium, his knee would ache.

"How is your leg feeling?"

Vincent shrugged.

"Have you changed your mind about Billycan after all that's happened? I mean, he saved your life that night. He saved all our lives. His change for the better . . . it was *real*, don't you think?"

Vincent let out a long breath and took a seat on the edge of a stack of journals. "I'm thankful to be alive." He smiled. "To be here with *you*. But it still doesn't wipe away what he did—to my family and so many others."

"Of course not," said Clover. "I just wonder how much blame you can put on someone who was under the control of something else. Those stories about his supernatural powers, his ability to possess rats, force them under his control. It turns out *he* was the one who was possessed. *He* was the one under the control of that terrible drug from the Topsiders' lab."

"I *know* you're right," Vincent finally said. "I suppose it feels like I'm betraying my family's memory by being even a little understanding of what happened to him. As though I'm saying their deaths meant nothing."

"No one thinks that," she replied softly. "Your family wouldn't think that." Clover took Vincent's chin in her paw and held it gently, forcing him to look her in the eyes. "Vincent, what would your father do? What would Julius Nightshade do?"

Vincent smiled wanly at her. "He'd forgive him."

"In the name of the Saints!" roared Juniper, just dodging a silver dagger as it whizzed by his snout.

"Oh dear!" said Texi, covering her heart with a trembling paw. "Juniper, are you all right?"

Juniper walked up to the wooden target affixed to the wall and wrenched out the dagger that had landed dead center. Taking a deep breath, he regarded the blade. "I'm fine," he said, looking back at the wall. "Your target, on the other hand, has seen better days. I thought you were old Batiste after my head as a Hallowtide treat." He grinned, nodding toward the door of the Council Chamber. "For everyone's sake, lock this door from now on if you're practicing, all right? I've only one eye left and I'd like to keep it, if you don't mind."

Texi suddenly gasped. "Juniper, your arm, you're wounded!"

"No worries," said Juniper, staring at the gash. "Vincent and I had a slight disagreement with an ill-tempered raccoon." He chuckled. "If you think this is bad, you should see the raccoon."

"Were you looking for the lost Hunters again? Did you discover anything?"

"Only to steer clear of raccoons brandishing apples, I'm afraid." He handed Texi her dagger. "You've become rather an impressive shot. I daresay you might give Vincent and Victor a run for their money."

"Elvi has me practicing day and night," replied Texi proudly.

Juniper cocked his head. "Why is she having you work on your defense skills?"

"She says it's good for my confidence."

"I suppose." Juniper looked Texi up and down. She'd changed. She was certainly more self-assured, and for that he was glad. After she'd helped Killdeer's insane sisters kidnap little Julius, her punishment had been to shadow Elvi, to be her apprentice. Texi had taken to Elvi's ways like a fish to water, even wearing a little black cloak just like her mentor's. No longer meek and seemingly slow-minded, as many had pegged her, Texi had become a smaller version of Elvi. Juniper wasn't sure how he felt about that. He wanted Texi to find out who *she* was, not imitate someone else. Then again, she *was* doing much better, bolder, more confident, just as he and Mother Gallo had hoped. Everyone had noticed the change.

"Elvi said it's vital that a rat know how to protect herself," added Texi, staring down at the blade. "She said one never knows what can happen." Her eyes widened. "There are enemies *all* around us, and sometimes those enemies are staring you right in the face—you just don't know it."

Juniper's brow furrowed. "I've never known Elvi to take such a dark view of things, but then again, all those years she spent in Tosca ... She was around your age when she was forced onto that boat during the Great Flood. She wasn't prepared for what life had in store for her, surviving in that jungle on her own. Luckily, she made it out alive."

"To be strong in mind, one must be strong in body," Texi recited.

"I suppose Elvi said that, too."

Nodding her head, Texi glanced at his wounded arm. "Juniper, do you think we'll ever find the lost Hunters?"

"I don't know," he replied gravely. "But I'll find them or die trying. Everyone on the Council is trying to figure out where they might be. Speaking of the Council, Ulrich misses you."

"I haven't seen him for a while. Elvi said I mustn't. Not until I learn all my life lessons. That's what she calls them, life lessons." She smiled weakly. "I do miss him, though. Ulrich always makes me laugh ... that stubby tail of his."

"Well," said Juniper, rapping his claws against his chin, "let me speak to Elvi. You've come a long way this past year." He patted Texi's shoulder. "I think it's high time you had a little diversion. Besides, we're all sick to death of Ulrich's constant grousing."

"Oh"—Texi looked down at her feet—"it's all right. You don't have to do that for me."

"But I *want* to," said Juniper.

"But after what I did . . . to . . . to little Julius, I don't think I should do anything but study for now, learn to be . . . good."

Juniper lifted Texi's chin. "My dear, you *are* good. All has been forgiven. We are not angry with you. Why, we never were. Maddy and I know how very hard you've been working . . . and how far you've come. You're stronger, more self-assured. Even your eyes—they shine brighter than before."

Texi placed the dagger back in the holster on her leg. The same kind Elvi had. "Thank you," she said softly.

Batiste was killed on Hallowtide Night,
while searching Topside for sweet delight.
Batiste was killed at quarter past three,
while searching for food in the Battery.
Now he is lonely, now he is dead,
now he Pennies-and-Pranks for your tail and your head!

The morbid verse ran through Billycan's head as he placed a grimacing gourd with a fanged mouth in a corner. There weren't any pumpkins to be found, so instead he and a band of others had absconded with a crate of small squashes they pinched from one of the many vendors at Tosca's open market. They'd do just fine.

After insisting the others go to bed, he and Ajax worked furiously through the night. When he thought about it, it sounded preposterous. Two grown rats who'd seen more war, death, and destruction than any creature should ever witness, sitting on the floor, surrounded by gourds and colored paper, whittling Jack-o'-lanterns and hanging cutouts of devils and spooks. He supposed it was fitting. It was *something*, in any case. It was yet another happy moment, another *good* moment, to help force out all the bad ones . . . the ones that haunted him far worse than any Hallowtide ghost ever could.

"They will be horrified!" he shouted as he made a frenzied dash down another corridor. He had planned everything so well. His white snout highlighted by firelight, he would start with the story of Batiste. He couldn't wait to tell the little ones of Tosca all about the aged phantom, roaming the corridors for Pennies-or-Pranking, searching aimlessly for his stolen sweets! His heart raced in anticipation. He hadn't felt this kind of rush in ages . . . not since that night . . . He shook his head vehemently. He didn't want to think about that. Not right now. No dark thoughts. Not today.

After hanging the last decoration, he stormed into the throne room just in time to find Ajax finishing up the face of a particularly demonic yellow squash. The black rat dropped a small candle inside it and lit it, raising a critical eyebrow at the gourd's ghastly yellow grin.

Ajax turned and stared at Billycan, who leaned against the doorway, catching his breath. "What? You don't like it?" asked Ajax. He folded his arms and sighed with frustration. "Too scary?"

Billycan's eyes brightened to an intense ruby in the candle's flickering light. His chest still heaving, his voice came out as a raspy whisper. "Just scary enough."

Juniper smiled as he watched Julius and Nomi zip around the breakfast table, Nomi intent on catching her brother's tail. The older boys, Tuk and Gage, had gone off with Mother Gallo to

Nightshade Passage already, eager to get a look at the latest batch of diaries recovered from the swamp.

Hob, still finishing his porridge, watched thoughtfully as Julius and Nomi fell headlong into the pillows surrounding the fire pit, giggling hysterically. "Father," he said, his eyes wandering cautiously over to Juniper, "can I ask you something?"

Juniper regarded the young rat, who poked at his porridge with a spoon. "What is it, my boy?" He winked at Hob. "You're not getting out of finishing your breakfast, if that's what you're after."

"No, that's not it," said Hob. His voice dropped to a whisper. "Father, we all know Billycan is Julius's father."

"Yes," said Juniper.

"Well . . . what I'm wondering is, who is Julius's . . . *mother*?"

Juniper eyed Julius as the little rat rolled cheerfully on the floor, his white hairs shedding on the pillows. "We haven't a clue. Billycan disappeared before we could ask him."

"Does Julius ever ask about her?"

"He asks about Billycan from time to time, wanting to make sure he's all right." Juniper shook his head, a part of him still amazed that the white rat—his brother—was no longer a mortal threat. "I think Julius is content with the mother he has." He chuckled. "Why, Maddy all but smothers that boy with affection!"

Hob wrinkled his nose, thinking. "But, Father, what if Julius's mother is bad, just like Billycan? What then?"

"I've thought about that, and it's entirely possible—birds of a feather, as they say—but no one has come forth to claim Julius, good, bad, or otherwise. I fear whoever Julius's mother is, she's long gone. Perhaps she ran away when the Catacombs citizens were freed. Perhaps she lives Topside now."

"How could she leave her own son?"

"That's hard to say. When I told our citizens the truth of what really happened here with Billycan last year, the cure, how it changed him, I think it gave them little relief. I, of all rats, certainly understand. Without proof, how could they not still think of him as the same fiend they knew back in the Catacombs—the brutal High Collector and Commander? I wanted to put their minds at ease, to assure them that he was no longer a threat, but without seeing his change with their own eyes, I cannot expect them to believe it." He shook his head. "Perhaps if they truly knew they were safe from him, Julius's mother would come forward. I've always wondered if she's hiding in Nightshade City, right under our very noses, simply too afraid of Billycan to come forward."

Hob studied his little brother with a gloomy expression. "Perhaps she's dead."

Juniper patted Hob's back. "Yes . . . sad to say, but perhaps she is."

"You're doing it!" said Elvi. "That's it, Texi!"

Texi's paw felt heavy as she flew at her would-be attacker, but she wielded her dagger nimbly, sticking the rat all the way up to the hilt. Growling intently, she pivoted in a taut circle and sliced it again, this time in the belly. As soon as the blade entered, she pulled it downward, gutting the rat in one solid motion. Her teeth clenched, she yanked the knife out, landing on her feet as she dropped to the ground.

"You've done it, Texi!" shouted Elvi, clapping her paws as she jumped up and down. "You've killed him!"

Panting furiously, Texi looked up at the burlap rat dangling from the ceiling of the deserted cell Billycan had once inhabited, now serving as her training room. She'd sliced the poor fellow stem to stern. Sand poured to the floor, covering her feet. She gasped, dropping her dagger to the ground. "I . . . did it?"

"Yes, darling, you did," said Elvi proudly, patting Texi's ginger head.

"But—but how could I?" asked Texi, mystified. "How did I jump that high?"

"Rats are accomplished jumpers, darling," Elvi replied. "You've been training for many months, not knowing your own strength. Your hard work has paid off."

"But . . . I'm so small, so slight. . . ."

Elvi wiggled a claw at her. "Now, now, my little soldier, what did I tell you about that sort of talk?"

Texi smiled shyly. "Don't belittle myself—ever. I've the spirit of a lion."

"Yes, my dear, the spirit of a lion from the deepest Toscan jungle, and the heart of a true warrior. You've come a very long way this past year." Texi's smile melted away.

"Why, what is it darling?" Elvi asked, concerned. "Why such a sad face, on such a triumphant occasion?"

"Oh," said Texi, "I'm not sad, really. I'm grateful . . . to you. You've done so much for me. You've always said we were sisters, but you're more like . . ." Her voice trailed off.

Elvi took Texi's paw in her own. "More like . . . a *mother*?"

"Yes," said Texi, lifting her chin. "I never knew my mother, but if I had, I'd want her to be just like you. You know, I'd do anything for you."

"Anything," repeated Elvi softly. She pulled down the hood of her cloak and embraced Texi. "Then, my dearest girl, your mother I shall be."

CHAPTER TWO

The Madness
of King Silvius

BARELY KEEPING HIS BALANCE on the edge of the stool, Ajax leaned forward, trying to reach the last of the Hallowtide decorations with a stick. He eyed Billycan tromping down the corridor with an armful of cutout ghouls and ghosts. "How on earth did you get this one so high?" he called out in a strained voice as he tried to stretch farther. "For goodness' sake, did you fly up here?"

Billycan laughed. "I think in my excitement I may have quite literally scaled the wall."

"Well," said Ajax, grunting as he jumped down from the stool, "you're taller than me." He offered the stick to Billycan. "Here, you try."

Cocking his head, Billycan stared blankly at the stick for a moment. His face went completely slack. His eyes flickered with recognition, shifting from crimson to a brilliant orange.

The stack of paper cutouts fell from his arm, spinning through the air and scattering about the corridor.

"What is it?" asked Ajax. "What's the matter?"

Still eyeing the stick, Billycan swallowed stiffly and took a cautious step forward. He pointed at it with a yellowed claw. His voice was guarded and taut. "Where . . . did you get *that*?"

"It belonged to the empress, our former leader." Ajax scoffed disdainfully. "I fetched it from the storeroom."

"What was her name, this empress?"

Ajax flared his nostrils and sneered. "Her name was Elvi." He looked at Billycan with concern. "You still haven't said . . . what's wrong? Why, you look like you've seen a ghost."

Billycan took the stick from Ajax, staring at the chipped black paint. It was an old one, one of his first, from the days before he and Killdeer took over the Catacombs. He wrapped his digits around it, feeling the cool handle. It felt comfortable, like reuniting with an old friend. His mind flashed back to the past, back to the nightmare that had been his life. Familiar scents came back to him, scents of those dead and buried, and scents of those whose black hearts brimmed with nothing but rancor and revenge. He felt ill to his core. "A ghost I could contend with. This is something far more deadly, I fear. I should have known." His body went rigid. "Show me the rest of her things. I need to see them."

"But . . . why?" asked Ajax. "Her reign was a wretched time in our history! She brought over a decade of despair to every rat in Tosca—to my family. She and her lot invaded our peaceful home, starved us, enslaved us—"

"Her *lot*?" asked Billycan, cutting him off.

"Yes." Ajax's face tightened. "She did not come here alone. She had a swarm of male cohorts with her."

Billycan exhaled heavily, trying to control himself. "Take

me to her things now." He set a jittery paw on Ajax's shoulder. "I promise, my friend . . . I'll explain everything to you later. Now, please, take me there."

"Follow me, then." Ajax turned and strode down the hall.

Without a word, Billycan reached up toward the ceiling of the corridor, clawing down the last decoration. Holding the stick Ajax had given him, he smashed his fist into the wall. He glanced down, snorting at his bloodied knuckles. His billy club was unscathed.

Sitting on a crate in a musty storeroom, Billycan pored over Elvi's former belongings. All around him were piles of exotic silks, velvets, and linens, trunks filled with ornate silver and gold cutlery, goblets, and necklaces, encrusted with jewels. He picked up a red silk cloak, etched with gold thread, its collar adorned with fine obsidian stones. It dangled from his claw as he regarded it. "Such finery," he said. "Not to my taste."

"When she left the island, there was no easy way to take her things with her, so she was forced to leave them here," said Ajax, fingering a pile of silk. "Our kingdom was once a beautiful place. We *all* shared in its splendor. She took that from us, forced us into slavery, turned rats I once considered friends into our jailers." He snorted. "I wanted to give the Toscans peace of mind after she left, and I was worried that the sight of her extravagant possessions would only dredge up constant memories of the suffering she caused. I thought hiding away all her things would somehow make us all forget, but even after all this time, her shadow still lingers."

"Even in my darkest days, I never believed in such trappings," recalled Billycan. "I left that up to the High Minister . . . Killdeer."

Ajax scratched his head. "That name . . . I've heard it before, from the empress herself."

Billycan exhaled with regret. His mind slipped back to the seaside warehouse where he and Killdeer plotted with their army to overthrow Trilok. And *she* was there, sitting among them, hanging on Killdeer's every word, the only female major among a sea of males, a high major to be exact, and the only female Killdeer respected, a female so crafty and cunning, always listening, always learning.

"The lot you said she came with," asked Billycan, pulling himself back to the present, "who were they?"

"At first she passed them off as refugees, same as her. She said they jumped a boat, escaping a fatal flood in Trillium, but they were actually her criminal associates . . . deadly ones at that."

"More of Killdeer's majors, I'm afraid . . . *my* majors, as was she."

"Lucky for us, they left the island with her, along with the Toscan rats who betrayed us."

"How many rats were with her when she left?" asked Billycan.

"A small army, enough to overpower us, and we are no small kingdom."

Billycan pulled anxiously at the hair on the sides of his head. "She used the name Elvi when she returned to Trillium. It was the name of a rat who had been a childhood friend of my brother's. She claimed to have been lost in Tosca all these years. Her real name is Hecate." Billycan tossed the garish cloak to the floor and got to his feet. Growling, he kicked a silver serving tray across the room. He paced in an agitated circle. "I *knew* she'd fled to Tosca, but only to save her own skin from the flood! I thought she'd merely been stranded here—alone. It never occurred to me she'd taken control, building herself an army! I thought the lost majors died in the flood, that she was the lone survivor." His shoulders slumped. He thought back to that night in the Catacombs when he said good-bye to Juniper, leaving his son with him, certain he'd be protected. I've made a grave mistake in judgment, he thought. Juniper could easily handle one vengeful rat, but a pack of Killdeer's majors and disloyal Toscans . . . even with his Council, he *won't* be prepared. Billycan ran a paw down the length of his snout, remembering calling out to Juniper, the Catacombs collapsing around them. Had Juniper heard his warning over the thunderous noise? I left too soon, he thought. At the time it seemed right. I only wanted to do *something* right, for once in my life!

Ajax sighed. "I knew she and those battle-worn brutes she came with were up to no good, but Silvius would not listen. He took to Elvi immediately—treated her like a daughter. She acted so sweet and vulnerable around him. Silvius was too kind for his own good."

"Silvius?"

"Yes, the rat who led Tosca for nearly two decades. He built our kingdom into a wonderful place . . . much like you described Nightshade City, much like that." Ajax bowed his head. "She befriended King Silvius, became his protégée, and then . . . she poisoned him. She was horrid, constantly testing her vile potions on innocent Toscan rats. She terrified them. They *believed* in black magic. They thought Elvi—Hecate—was a sorceress, and she was only too eager to prove them right. Silvius never saw her treachery." He sighed again.

"I'm sorry about Silvius. Hecate is not beyond murder," said Billycan. "In fact, she's rather a practiced hand at it."

He looked down at his scarred torso, remembering how she attacked him in his cell. "She nearly killed me."

"I should explain," said Ajax. "Silvius. He isn't dead."

Billycan's hackles rose. "You mean this Silvius is *alive*? He's in Tosca?"

"Yes, he's here, only . . ."

"Only what?"

"He's a bit, well, what's the best way to put it? He's . . . mad."

Ajax led Billycan to an older part of the Toscan underground kingdom, a place were few rats still dwelled.

Billycan eyed the vacant quarters as they walked down the lonely corridor. "It seems sound, perfectly livable here." He knocked on a wall. "What reason would rats have to desert this corridor? We've little space as it is." As if on cue, a bloodcurdling howl followed by a cursing male voice bounced off the walls of the corridor. Both rats halted in their tracks.

"That would be your reason," said Ajax.

"King Silvius, I presume," said Billycan.

"Indeed."

"I see," said Billycan, gritting his teeth. "I was hoping Silvius could assist us, give us more information on Hecate—anything helpful, any plan she might have mentioned."

"It was Hecate who caused his madness, with her poisons," said Ajax as they reached a thick wooden door. "I'm afraid Silvius will give you a great deal of information, heaps of it in fact, just not the kind you're looking for."

"Brilliant," said Billycan dryly, pulling on his whiskers. Scattered mutterings came from the other side of the door. When Ajax had said "mad" Billycan had hoped for mere senility, the confusion of old age, not actual insanity. It seemed a conversation with this aging king would be for nothing.

Ajax knocked softly. "Silvius," he said in the mildest of tones, "it's Ajax, come for a visit." The muttering swiftly stopped. "I've brought a friend along, quite an interesting fellow. He'd love to meet you, and I reckon you two would have much to talk about." Still silence. "He's from Trillium . . . like you."

The muttering started again, only this time louder and more chaotic, as if the rat was deeply agitated. The heavy iron lock was unlatched from the other side of the door. Behind his back Billycan readied his claws, unsure of what to expect from this demented, raving rat.

Slowly the door creaked open. A tall rat stood in the doorway, his head nearly grazing the ceiling.

Billycan's mouth dropped wide open. He stared at the rat, speechless. His palms grew wet and his heart thundered as his eyes met those of the beloved Toscan king.

The rat stared back at him and chuckled. He curled his oversized paws into fists, resting them on his hips, as he gave Billycan the once-over. "You know what they say, don't you? You best close your mouth, lad, lest you want to catch flies."

Silvius patted Ajax's shoulder warmly as he stepped into the corridor. "Ajax, always fine to see you, though I wish you'd come more often." The aging rat was tall, big-boned, but lean, verging on skeletal. He wore a threadbare robe the color of plums. Despite his tattered attire, and patches of his fur that were yellowed with age, there was a regal air about him. "Ajax says you're from Trillium, then?" he asked Billycan. "Is that right?"

"Y-Yes," stammered Billycan.

The rat clapped his paws together. "Wonderful! Just wonderful. Come in, come in. We've so much to talk about, you and I, so much indeed!" He waved a long arm, motioning Billycan and Ajax inside. "Tea, tea, I must put on some tea!" He hurried ahead of them. "Where is that blasted pot?" Billycan watched in silence as Silvius tore through his things, documents, quill pens, and assorted objects flying through the air.

Ajax nudged Billycan. "What's come over you?" he whispered. "I've never seen you at such a loss for words."

"Why—why didn't you mention Silvius was from Trillium?"

Ajax shrugged. "Silvius has been here for decades. I didn't think it mattered."

"Well, then, why didn't you mention he was an—"

"Come along, gentleman," called Silvius, gesturing toward the fireplace with a chipped teapot. "Bad tea and good conversation await!"

"He's in a fine mood today," said Ajax. "When he's like this, he likes to talk—as you can see. If you want any information about Hecate that makes any sense, we best get to it."

When he'd seen his son for the first time, Billycan had been amazed. He'd looked at little Julius, and it was as though he were looking into a mirror, a vision of himself, only a great deal smaller. Intently, Billycan watched Silvius as the old rat extended a long, snow-white arm, grasping the fire poker in his tarnished yellow claws, his crimson eyes glinting off the dying embers. The little mirror image Billycan had seen in Julius had suddenly grown full size.

Silvius was not exaggerating when he said *bad* tea. Apart from its burnt aftertaste, it was watery and flat, though tea was the last thing on Billycan's mind. He glanced around the mildewed quarters as Ajax filled Silvius in on recent Toscan happenings. The room was a shambles. Ink-stained quills and crumpled papers were strewn about. Crates of rolled-up parchments and documents of all shapes and sizes were stacked in crooked towers all the way up to the ceiling; others were piled on any available shelf, stool, or dresser. Ajax and Billycan managed to clear off two armchairs near the fire.

The walls, once covered in fine cloth, had been painted black; drawings, words, and diagrams in white chalk scrolled across them, crowding together, forming a jumbled sea of frenzied thoughts and shapes.

Silvius stood as he spoke, pitching his arms passionately, as though every word had profound meaning. "Hallowtide!" he declared after Ajax told him of their little celebration for the children. Abruptly he held an offended paw to his chest and gave Ajax a wounded look. "And why was _I_ not invited? Surely the children would have delighted in my presence."

With a visible gulp, Ajax said evenly, "We didn't want to keep you from . . . your work." He nodded toward the muddle of words snaking across the walls. "We know how important it is, and your time—it's so valuable." He looked at Silvius expectantly, his expression an odd mix of dread and hope.

Silent for a long moment, Silvius finally said, "Oh. Well of course!" Ajax exhaled. "My findings are quite pressing. I can't be frolicking with little ones when there is work to be done." His eyes twinkled. "Why, I haven't thought of Hallowtide in decades. What a delicious, albeit creepy, occasion—stealing candy, scaring the life out of one another! What fun I used to have back in Trillium, skulking about, pretending to be Batiste. Oh, the days. . . ."

Billycan studied Silvius from his chair. "That's my birthday," he said, almost in a whisper. "I was born on Hallowtide."

Silvius cocked his head, his left ear drooping slightly. His eyes widened. He regarded Billycan with a strange air. "Were you?" he asked.

"Yes . . . in a lab, in Trillium." Billycan mustered a thin smile, hoping his comment didn't spark questions about the lab, the shots . . . his mother. He tried to change the topic. "When did you leave Trillium?"

Scratching his chin, Silvius leaned against the fireplace mantel, nearly setting the edges of his robe ablaze. "Probably before you were born," he finally said. He shook his head rapidly. "In fact, I'm sure I had left Trillium by then. I'm far older than you, to be sure." He leaned in, inspecting Billycan's face. "How old *are* you? You're battle-worn without a doubt, but by no means an old mossback like me!" He laughed. "Did you know, most rats pay little attention to their years in this world? Come to think of it, I can't recall a single Toscan who's mentioned his birthday."

"I'm—"

Before Billycan could answer, Silvius snatched up a filthy mirror lying atop a stack of ragged maps and regarded himself. He yanked up a side of his mouth and inspected his ruddy gums and graying teeth. "I'm not entirely certain how old *I* am either, but I'm over one hundred, to be sure."

Billycan needed no further convincing that Silvius was indeed insane. Not even a Trillium rat could reach that age. Furthermore, this rat looked younger than Trilok, and he was in his seventies at the time of his demise—an age considered ancient among Trillium rats. What a pity, he thought, his hopes of finding out more about Hecate dying. "Surely you must be mistaken," he replied as mildly as possible. "Years like that rarely come to *humans*. They certainly don't come to the likes of us."

"Oh, pish-posh," said Silvius, waving a dismissive paw. "I may not know my *exact* year of birth, but I'm most positively over one hundred years of age. Of that I am certain."

"You can't possibly be that old," Billycan insisted. "Yes, rats of our kind do live long lives, leaps and bounds longer than ordinary rats, but to live a century? Why, it's not possible—not in the least."

Suddenly Silvius lunged forward. He loomed over Billycan, trapping him in his chair, and glared at him snout to snout. "Is that so, *rat*?"

Ajax jumped to his feet. "It's all right, Silvius," he said in a soothing tone. He patted Silvius's shoulder, gently pulling him back. "Billycan means no harm, none at all. He's merely stating facts as he knows them." He grinned sheepishly at the former king. "He's entitled to his opinion, just as you are."

"His *opinion* is far from *fact*," declared Silvius, grimacing at them both. "It's pure ignorance!"

Billycan bolted from his chair. He had been called many things in his lifetime, but ignorant was not one of them. "Then educate me, *King* Silvius," he said disdainfully. His eyes shifted to a scorching amber, his rage rising inside him. He gritted his teeth, forcing himself not to claw the old rat's eyes out. "Explain to me—clearly a stupid rat who's *never* known any creature, Trillium-born or otherwise, to live even close to one hundred years—tell me how it's possible!" Silvius growled, glowering indignantly. Billycan poked Silvius in the chest. "I said, *tell* me!"

"Gentlemen, please," said Ajax. "Control your tempers!"

Snarling, Silvius snatched up his teacup from the mantel and hurled it into the fire. Porcelain shards scattered across Billycan's feet. Froth formed at the corners of Silvius's mouth as he spoke. "Very well, I'll tell you! Blast it all, I'll *show* you!" He cursed under his breath, motioning with a wide sweep of his arm to the walls and ceiling. "I admit, whatever *she* gave me, it has damaged my mind." He pulled wildly on his ears. "It eats away at my memories!" He kicked a pile of books across the room. "Why do you think I write it all down, for Saints' sake, taking up every spare inch of my quarters? To remember!"

Silvius's tone took Billycan by surprise. He didn't sound confused or nonsensical, he sounded desperate and committed to what he was saying—as though he'd stake his life on his claim. Billycan's anger subsided as he saw the bleak look on Silvius's face. "You're lucky she didn't kill you," he said. "When I knew her, Hecate rarely made mistakes." He pointed to the long scar on his torso. "It seems we were both lucky."

"Hecate," whispered Silvius, taking an unsteady breath. "I thought her name was Elvi. Of course she wouldn't use her real name."

Billycan nodded. "I knew her back in Trillium. There was a time when I respected Hecate, even trusted her with my life." He remembered how easily she controlled the male ràts she commanded, how afraid of her they'd been. "She's wicked to her very core."

"Was she held captive in the lab, too?"

"No, I'm afraid the humans had nothing to do with the evil inside her. Even in her younger days, her malice was legendary."

"You escaped the lab—Prince Pharmaceuticals—during the fire, did you not?" asked Silvius, staring blankly at the broken shards of his teacup that had landed in the fireplace. His gaze seemed trapped in some far-off place. "That fire . . . those of us who escaped with our lives, we were all very fortunate."

"What do you mean, *we*?" asked Billycan, his whole body rigid. "You were in the lab, weren't you?"

Silvius bowed his head. "Yes, I was . . . but that's one part of my history I'd prefer *not* to remember. Somehow, though, it's the only part I can't seem to forget. It seems you'd like to forget it as well."

"You were given the shots too, then," said Billycan.

"Back in the lab, they weren't just giving rats shots. They

were taking from us, too. I wasn't given shots. In that way, I was lucky. My torture involved something else entirely."

"What do you mean?"

Silvius pointed to Billycan's chair. "Please, sit."

Billycan's eyes drifted to the chalk-covered walls and ceiling. What he had thought was a madman's maze of scribbles began to take proper shape. He wasn't staring at the ravings of a lunatic. He hadn't recognized it at first; maybe he hadn't cared to. He was staring at a large map—a map of Trillium.

Evening had set in. Ajax snored in his chair. A place to rest his bones and a crackling fire were all that it took to put him fast asleep. Billycan was wide awake.

"Tell me," said Silvius, reclining in his chair. "Why did you come here—to Tosca?"

"To get away," Billycan replied. "I told you of my past. Staying in Trillium was a constant reminder of it. I thought I could do some good in Tosca, do *something*, at any rate. I'd heard of the harsh jungle conditions, the rough way of life here. . . . I can't erase what I've done, the pain I've caused so many that will never go away, but coming here—I thought in some small way, perhaps, I could do a little good."

"A very noble reason, young rat, but why did you come *here*? There are scores of places in the world where rats' lives are less than tolerable. Why did you choose this place over all others? What got you to this *precise* location?"

Billycan pondered the question. There *were* many other places he could have gone, and done just as much good, places much closer and easier to get to. "I—I don't know. Something just *drew* me here. I cannot explain it."

"All these rats"—Silvius nodded at Ajax, snoring softly in his chair—"the rats who so freely allowed you to lead them, just as they did me, they are descended from Trillium rats. Only they don't know it. Just as you were, their forefathers were driven to this island. Something inborn *impelled* them here, a compulsion they could not control."

"But what?" asked Billycan.

"That's what I'm trying to determine. Sadly, much of Tosca's history is lost. The tropical environment, the constant humidity have rotted away much of their written words. We tried our best to preserve what we could over the years, but our archives are nearly destroyed." Reaching into a wooden cask next to his chair, Silvius retrieved a large rolled-up parchment. "Here, take the other end."

Unrolling it together, he and Billycan gazed upon a faded map. The map depicted a portion of the vast Hellgate Sea, with three coastlines around it. "Here is the coast of Tosca," said Silvius, tapping it. He ran his claw all the way to the other side of the map. "And here is the coast of Mastiff County, the swamp you ended up in."

Billycan studied the center coastline. "Is this . . . Trillium?" Silvius nodded. "I never realized it was midway between Tosca and the swamp."

"Did you know Trillium sits on an ancient volcano?"

"Yes, I've heard that before."

Silvius pulled out another map from the cask, a smaller one. Unrolling it on top of the other, he tapped on the three coastlines of the Hellgate Sea and pointed to three red dots, one in Trillium, another in the swamp, and the last in Tosca. "Each red dot represents a volcano." He revealed more dots, farther away. "As you can see, volcanoes, extinct and otherwise, exist throughout our world, but Tosca's and Mastiff's volcanoes are the closet to Trillium."

"What does that matter to us?"

"I found an early Toscan document, something written by the Trillium rats who originally landed here." He pointed to a browned parchment pinned to the wall. "According to its translation, we once lived in the center of Trillium's extinct volcano. I think we're chasing something from that volcano. Something we can no longer find in Trillium—something hidden from us."

"But what?"

Silvius looked down at the map on his lap, tracing the small drawing of Trillium's City Museum with his claw. "The City Museum is built in the center of Trillium, the exact center of the volcano. And do you know what was next to the museum?" Billycan shook his head. "Our former home."

His ears perking, Billycan sat up in his chair. "You mean . . . the *lab*?"

Silvius smiled. "Good, lad. You're catching on. Not only was the lab next door, the buildings were connected—one and the same. The blaze was put out before it reached the museum."

"You said the Topsiders took something from you in the lab. What was it?"

Lifting his left leg, Silvius revealed a massive scar running along the inside, an area of his flesh that went concave as though carved out with a knife. "They took my flesh. They took my blood. Remarkably, they didn't take my soul, thank the Saints for that. Whatever changed us—made us bigger, stronger, better—they wanted it."

"But what was it? What were they after?"

Silvius traced a circle around the drawing of the museum. "Whatever makes a rat like me, a creature that should live no more than four or five years, live to over one hundred—that's what they were after, and I reason that if they haven't yet found it, they're still searching. The humans will always want more than they have. If whatever lies in the heart of that volcano is the reason for our extended lives, our strength and intelligence, just *think* of what it could do for a human."

"They could live forever," said Billycan.

Silvius's claw landed in the center of the map. "Whatever the answer is, I believe it is hidden in the museum."

CHAPTER THREE

Diaries Found in the Attic

THE COUNCIL HAD GATHERED over tea, trying to make sense of several diary entries. "When they found the above-ground city our ancestors had built, the scientists clearly knew we weren't ordinary rats," said Juniper. "Lucky for us that they were the ones who found us. As we all know, the Topsiders' world is full of those who hate rats."

"It seems the scientists were driven out of Trillium by the city's founders," said Virden. "According to this journal entry, they had gone to the then new government and tried to tell Trillium's leaders of our uniqueness, but politicians knew most humans would never want to live in a city of baffling, super-intelligent rats, so they forced the scientists out, denouncing them and threatening their lives."

"So the scientists fled," said Cole, setting down the last page of the journal, "taking cages full of Trillium rats with them. They say they stopped many places, but it was not until they got to the swamp that the rats seemed at ease again. Back in

Trillium, the rest of the rats took to hiding, driven underground to save their own lives."

"Indeed," said Virden, "the scientists stole away to the swamp so they could do their research in peace and safety. They built the manor themselves, turning it into one giant home for the scientists and their families."

Vincent smiled. "Like us."

"The diaries go back nearly a hundred years," added Carn, "and all are filled with the scientists' observations, such as how we share physical traits with humans—we sweat, our eyes make tears, things normal rats cannot do."

"Normal rats don't sweat?" asked Victor. "They don't shed tears?"

Suttor nudged him and covered his nose. "There have been many times when I wished you didn't sweat."

"One of the entries details how we communicated with the scientists through some sort of sign language," said Carn.

"Though we couldn't speak to them, we all understood each other," added Oleander.

Mother Gallo thought of little Ramsey, the Topsider boy who helped them the night Nightshade City was officially born. How easily he'd understood her.

Oleander got up from her chair and flipped through the journal on the Council table until she found a particular page. "Our ancestors used to sneak into the manor parlor, wanting to learn with the human children. They thought no one knew." She tapped a claw on the parchment. "Here, listen."

We've let the rats out on their own, giving them full run of the manor. They seem in no hurry to leave our company, but still curious to explore the new world around them. Almost every day, during the children's lessons, the rats slink into the parlor and silently gather under the davenport. They think we don't take notice of them, but we do—all twenty of them listening intently. Since we've let them roam as they please, their personalities are blossoming, each one as unique as our own children. With the help of an open window, Tar has taken to the roof, slipping in and out by way of the attic. Always staring up at the sky, he sits up there for hours. Coriander, well, she's quite the mischievous one. Cook has discovered her time and time again rummaging through the cupboards, cleverly mixing spices together, tasting each new concoction as if she's trying out recipes. Of course Cook has her doubts, but I deem any day now Coriander will waltz out of the kitchen carrying roast mutton and plum pudding with a most triumphant grin upon her face! Then there's wise Garrick, constantly searching the library, always with his nose sandwiched between pages of a book. Following a small illustration, he built a birdhouse out of twigs and stones he'd found in the yard. The house was remarkable, just like the one in the picture, yet my praise did come with a scolding. He knows he and the others are not allowed in the yard. The snakes would make a feast of them. I'm afraid one of these days we will lose one of our precious rats, their thirst for knowledge getting the better of them, but I dare not think about that right now. I simply cannot.

"We're still piecing things together," said Cole. "We have the swamp diaries, and they mention more diaries in the museum archives, but Virden and I were nearly caught trying to find them." He shook his head. "It's all a puzzle, especially the diary entry that claims we came from inside a volcano."

"We lived in an above-ground city back then," said Suttor. He glanced at the torches affixed to the wall. "I can't imagine living with constant daylight."

Virden nodded. "Well, when Trillium was still called

Brimstone, just a small, budding city, that's exactly what we did."

"I like the sound of that . . . 'Brimstone,' very mysterious," said Oleander.

"Brimstone, otherwise known as sulfur, is a product of volcanoes," said Virden. "The name was quite fitting at the time."

"It's all so remarkable," said Juniper. "The secrets of who we are, finally unfolding." He glanced at the Council. "Elvi, are you all right? You look like you're miles away."

Elvi shook her head as though coming out of a trance. "Oh," she said, "I was just thinking of a rat I used to know in Tosca. He would be very interested in our recent discoveries."

"Really, and who was that?"

"Just another ignorant Toscan with outlandish ideas. By now he's quite insane." A wisp of smile formed on her lips. "When I left Tosca things did not look good for him."

"What a pity," said Mother Gallo, patting Elvi's paw.

Clover cocked her head. "Are you sure, Elvi, that all the Toscans are as ignorant as you've always said?" She gazed thoughtfully at Oleander. "The bats always believed the swamp rats were that way, but plainly that was not the case."

"I suppose some could have *normal* intelligence," Elvi replied with a sniff, "but nothing like us." All eyes on her, she shifted awkwardly in her seat. She smiled around the table. "I do see your point, but I lived in Tosca for a good part of my life. I *know* the Toscan rats. They are *nothing* like us."

"We believe you, dear," offered Mother Gallo. "Our Clover likes to see the good in everyone."

Elvi raised a curious eyebrow. "Even Billycan?" she asked. "Do you see the good in him?"

"Yes," said Clover, nodding her head resolutely. "I do. That night in the Catacombs, when we were surrounded by

Killdeer's loathsome sisters, the old Billycan would have killed us without hesitation, as the first step in regaining control . . . but he didn't." She glanced at Vincent and Victor. "As far back as any of us can remember, Billycan hated everything about Julius Nightshade. And now I have Billycan to thank for keeping Julius Nightshade's and Uncle's dream alive . . . for keeping *all* of us alive."

"Well said, my dear," said Juniper.

Rolling her eyes, Elvi muttered under her breath, "Next thing you know she'll be calling him *Uncle* Billycan."

Mother Gallo's ears perked up at the remark.

There was a knock at the door. "It's him," said Suttor, rising to his feet.

Suttor opened the door to a sizable rat with fur the color of carrots. Once a chubby fellow, Suttor's little brother had thinned out. He was now a strapping young rat with a strong, square jaw, broad shoulders, and muscles to spare.

"Duncan," said Juniper, "thank you for coming." Juniper had a fondness for Duncan. After all, it was he who had told the Council about the Topside chimneys that led down to the Kill Army kitchen in the Catacombs—an instrumental part in Nightshade's victory.

Glancing timidly around the room, Duncan nodded at the Council. Though he was much older now, he was still a daydreamer.

Shrinking down in her chair, Elvi pulled the hood of her cloak farther down over her face until only her snout was visible. She folded her arms around herself and hid her paws in her sleeves. Mother Gallo nudged her softly. "Elvi, what's got into you today?" she whispered.

"Everyone, young Duncan has an interesting story," said

Juniper. "When he was a boy, living in the Catacombs, he had quite an adventure in the Trillium City Museum."

"After our parents died," said Suttor, "and before the Kill Army had come to round us up, Duncan ran off. He slipped past the guard at our sector's exit, who was preoccupied with another citizen, and set off Topside on his own."

"You're lucky you were not seen by the guard. He would have skinned you alive," said Ulrich.

"It was a foolish thing to do," said Duncan. "I know."

"How did you survive Topside all alone, lad?" asked Ragan. "It's dangerous enough for a full-grown rat."

"I found my way to the city museum quite by accident. I lived there for about a week until I decided to come home." Duncan sighed longingly. "I—I loved it there. It was so different from the gloomy Catacombs, so much to explore."

"And you still remember it," asked Virden, "after all this time?"

Cole smiled proudly at his adopted son. "Duncan's memory is as sharp as a tack when it comes to that museum. I wish I'd known he knew the place so well *before* you and I set out on our little investigation last year."

"Agreed," said Virden. "The museum is near impossible to navigate without a map of some sort. Your help will be most valuable, Duncan."

"I'll gladly guide you through the museum," said Duncan. "I wanted to take my brothers back to the museum after I returned, but the army quickly rounded us up. There was something special about that place—and more than just the fact that it was far away from the Catacombs. If I hadn't missed my brothers so much, I never would have left."

CHAPTER FOUR
Bed Bugs

BILLYCAN ENTERED THE STOREROOM as if his worst enemy waited inside. His mind raced back to the Bloody Coup. He'd carried out his plan with ease that night, but he remembered wondering at the time where Hecate was.

How naturally High Major Hecate had taken to his ways! Before Hecate, Billycan never valued the few females who had joined Killdeer's ranks, but she changed all that. His eyes flashed with twisted approval as he recalled her talent for torture. She'd enjoyed it just as much as he did, possibly more. How effortlessly she'd killed, a deft hand with both sword and dagger.

"The blasted flood!" he shouted. He slashed at the golden tapestries that covered the walls, shredding them to ribbons, carving the wall with deep claw marks. "It ruined all my plans for her!"

Certainly the Great Flood had many benefits at the time.

It was the event that had allowed them to take over the Catacombs. It had covered up his crimes that night, too—the murder of Julius Nightshade and his wretched wife and children. If only he'd gotten to those scrawny brothers sooner, before they could escape! Hecate was supposed to be by his side that night, taking the lead! Vincent and Victor would have been hacked to pieces along with their Loyalist father. They never would have escaped! How different everything would have been. Before he saw her back in Nightshade, he'd thought she'd simply been stranded in Tosca all this time since the flood—but no! She'd been plotting, scheming, ruling a kingdom, dripping with silk and jewels. "Garish little shrew! Selfish little fiend!" he screamed.

"The little traitor snake, with her lying serpent tongue!" Billycan roared, his wrathful shrieks growing louder with every word. He scrambled up a stack of crates and grabbed for the velvet curtains that hung from the ceiling, swinging across the room as he ripped them to the ground.

His chest burned. He couldn't breathe. Panting, Billycan grabbed his knees and put his head down, thinking his heart might burst if he couldn't catch his breath. As he looked up he caught his reflection in the mirror. He stared intently at himself. Foam dripped from his mouth down his chest. His teeth were bared, ready to rip out the throat of anyone who might dare cross his path. His eyes glowed an acrid copper. The sight made him smile.

Dragging himself to his feet, Ajax stretched his body, every muscle stiff after sleeping in a chair all night. He took a step back and stared at Billycan and Silvius, his eyes darting between the two. They'd both fallen asleep in their chairs in identical positions, the left leg swung over the right, their arms folded neatly across their chests. Even their heads were in the same position, both upright against their chairs and leaning to the same side. But for the marked difference in age and the black scar on Billycan's snout, he'd have had a hard time telling them apart. He cleared his throat.

Billycan quickly roused, his red eyes coming into focus. He rubbed his brow and craned his neck. "Silvius and I were up most of the night, talking. He thinks Hecate had been poisoning him long before she took over Tosca, clouding his thoughts with something she put in the tea."

"It makes perfect sense. She was always experimenting with herbs and plants from the jungle, testing her vile concoctions on unsuspecting rats," Ajax said irritably. "By the way, where did you go last night?"

Yawning, Billycan cracked his neck. "Nowhere. I was here all night."

"But . . . I saw you. You stormed out in a rage. I reasoned Silvius had said something that set you off."

Billycan shook his head. "I fell asleep sometime after Silvius." He picked up a map that had fallen to the floor at his feet. "I was studying this."

Ajax scratched his head. "Hmm . . . perhaps I dreamed it. Yesterday was a strange day, after all." He looked at Silvius. "This is the strongest I've seen him in some time. After Hecate took control, she had him locked up in a cell, told everyone he'd gone mad with jungle fever, that we were in mortal danger if we allowed him to be free. I knew better—most of us did— but we were helpless against her henchmen. They threatened harm to our children if we did not conform." Ajax snarled. "I should have been stronger. She blew into Tosca, weaseling her way into Silvius's good graces. Before I knew it, it was too late.

I've faced down jungle beasts all my life, but against her and her nasty band of rats I was helpless. We all were."

"You were right to obey her. I doubt you'd be breathing right now, had you not. As for her tea, it's clear now how she's fooled Juniper and his Council." Billycan gazed at Silvius as he slept. "I have to stop Hecate from whatever revenge she has planned for Juniper and the others before it's too late." He felt his throat, remembering the lab tag that had existed there for so many years of his life. "There's something else I need to do . . . for me"—he nodded at Silvius—"and for him."

"You can't just pick up and leave, you know."

"You Toscans are self-sufficient. You don't need me to lead you."

"The Toscans like having you. You bring them happiness, just as Silvius did in his day."

"*You* should be leading them, not me. They've known you all their lives. They trust you."

Ajax bowed his head. "I was a makeshift leader, I suppose, after Hecate left, but I felt guilty about what she had done to us. I still do. I should have thought of a way to defeat her. Instead I allowed her to enslave us." He sighed. "You remind me of Silvius, in more ways than mere looks. You told me the truth about your past, and though those who knew you then may disagree, you are kind. Generous." He smiled. "If *you* are deceiving us, you're a far better liar than Hecate ever was. I saw the cracks in her story from the very first day she arrived. With luck the Nightshade rats will have seen her true colors by now, too."

Billycan could only hope Ajax was right and Hecate had finally revealed the wicked rat she really was and been locked up, unable to do harm. She had never been known for her patience. How much longer would she wait?

* * *

Except for the original members, the Council had dispersed. Suttor, Duncan, and Kar made their way back to their quarters after stopping in the library to get some studying in.

"Duncan, you did well in the Council meeting," said Suttor. "You've always wanted to do more for Nightshade. Now you can."

"Lali will be happy," said Kar, Suttor and Duncan's little brother.

Under his orange fur, Duncan reddened at his brothers' approval. "Thanks," he said. "I can't wait to visit the museum again." He looked distant for a moment. "But it will remind me of Mother and Father."

"Don't be gloomy," said Suttor. "You're going to help all of Nightshade City. Mother and Father would be so proud of you."

"They can see us," added Kar in a whisper. "Lali says they're up with the Saints, watching over us."

"Without a doubt," said Suttor. "They are up there, making sure we're all right. It's a miracle we're all still alive. I think Mother and Father had a hand in keeping us safe."

"I still hear their voices sometimes," said Duncan. "When I'm all alone, I swear I can hear them talking, especially Mother."

"I don't remember what they sounded like," said Kar, far too young at the time of their death to recall much about his parents.

"Mother had a soft voice," said Suttor, "like alfalfa honey. She sang a lot, too—better than any rat I've ever heard."

"Father was funny," said Duncan, "and when he laughed, it would fill up our whole quarters."

"Yes," said Suttor. "He had a booming voice that would shake the walls of the Catacombs!"

Kar looked down shyly, glad to be with his brothers. Staring at his empty paws, he suddenly realized that something was missing. "My books!" he said urgently. "I left them in the library again! Lali will be furious!"

"Calm down," said Suttor. "We'll go get them, problem solved."

Suttor ruffled Duncan's bushy orange fur, just able to reach the top of his towering brother's head. As they reached their quarters, Suttor said, "You stay here. If Lali or Cole comes home, tell them I was helping Kar finish up his studies and we'll be back shortly."

"See, Kar, they'll be none the wiser," said Duncan. "That's what brothers are for."

"Yes, to cover your back!"

"Come on, then," said Suttor. "The library closes soon."

Duncan unlocked the door and entered his family's quarters. Striking a match against the wall, he lit the nearest candle, carrying it over to the kitchen table. His bed caught his eye. He didn't remember leaving the covers in such an awful mess. He would have sworn he'd made it this morning, but with the excitement of the Council, he'd probably forgotten. "Silly rat," he said to himself.

He sat down on the edge of the bed, happy to be home. "Duncan . . .," said a dreamy voice, "is that you?"

Duncan's eyes widened and his hackles rose. He jumped up from the bed and whipped around. "Who's there?" he demanded, eyeing the room for some sort of weapon.

"Goodness," said the bleary voice, "I didn't mean to frighten you."

She was so small, Duncan hadn't noticed a rat was in his bed. He saw tiny gray feet peeking out from under his quilt, and the edges of a black cloak. "Elvi?"

Pushing back the quilt, Elvi sat up and rubbed her face tiredly.

"What—what are you doing here?" asked Duncan. "Sleeping in my bed."

"Oh dear," said Elvi, stretching, "I didn't mean to fall asleep and startle you so. After the Council meeting, I came to see Lali. The door was unlocked, so I decided to wait inside, thinking she'd be back soon from Bostwick Hall." She wrung her paws. "I've been so tired lately, I sat down on your bed and the next thing I knew your voice woke me up."

Duncan retrieved a mug from the cupboard, filling it with bitonberry juice from the pitcher on the table. He'd noticed Elvi had been gloomy lately. Everyone had. He felt bad for her. She had no family to call her own and sometimes seemed so out of place in Nightshade. "Here," he said, handing her the mug. "This always wakes me up."

"Such a good boy," said Elvi after taking a long drink, "you and your brothers, all such gentlemen. After all you three lads have been through, you still have such generous hearts." She sighed. "Speaking of your brothers, how is Suttor doing? He's got so much responsibility now—a respected Council member, a guard in the prison corridor. When does he find time to sleep?"

"Trust me, he sleeps," said Duncan, taking a seat at the table. He smiled. "He always wakes me up with his snoring."

"I would snore too," said Elvi, "working every day in the prison corridor. It must be so tiring guarding all those prisoners day in and day out. How does he like it?"

"Well, I—I haven't really been to see him," said Duncan hesitantly.

"But why not?" asked Elvi, surprised.

Duncan looked down at his paws. "I don't like it there," he admitted. "It's eerie . . . all the former majors from the Kill Army, not to mention High Majors Schnauss and Foiber. I don't like how I feel when I'm there. It's creepy."

"I understand how you feel." Elvi got off the bed and sat next to Duncan at the table. She took down the hood of her cloak so Duncan could see her eyes. "Like I always tell Texi, we must be brave, even when we don't think we can be. And look how far she's come."

"But I'm not exactly what you'd call fearless," said Duncan.

"You don't need to be fearless in order to be brave," said Elvi. "Some of the bravest rats I know still get scared. It's only natural. Even after all those years fighting off beasts in the jungle of Tosca, I can still be frightened." She patted his shoulder. "I have an idea."

"What sort of idea?"

"Why don't you take your brother a nice pot of tea someday soon while he's working one of those tiring shifts? I'll be glad to brew it for you."

Duncan cocked his head, thinking. Elvi's tea *was* Suttor's favorite, and he did feel guilty for never visiting him. Still, he didn't like the idea of seeing the Kill Army majors. "Well, I—"

"Didn't you just tell the Council how you left the Catacombs all on your own?" Duncan nodded. "That you went up to Trillium and lived among the humans by yourself? Surely you can handle the majors, all locked up tight, unable to ever hurt anyone again. After all, you're not a little boy anymore."

Elvi was right. The more he thought about it, the more he felt like a coward. She faced down the Toscan jungle at his age, and here he was whining over rats who'd been safely behind bars for nearly four years now. "All right," he said decisively. "I'll do it."

"Oh, that's wonderful to hear," said Elvi. "Your brother will be so thankful to see your friendly face during a long, dreary day in the prison corridor. I'm sure your mother can spare a basket of her famous muffins for you, too."

"That would be nice," he said, genuinely excited about the idea. Though he never mentioned it, Duncan was sure Suttor knew of his fear of the prison corridor. He wanted Suttor to be proud of him.

"It's settled, then," said Elvi, rubbing her paws together. She grinned from ear to ear.

CHAPTER FIVE
Moments of Happiness

BILLYCAN HAD REOPENED Hecate's former throne room and turned it into a dining room of sorts for all of Tosca. Palm fronds of what could only be pure gold hung from the rafters of the opulent space, with matching gold vines spiraling down lofty marble pillars.

He'd found the storeroom in shambles, some of Hecate's things destroyed, as though a wild animal had gotten loose inside. He wondered if Ajax's temper had finally gotten the better of him. After all, he felt responsible for all that had happened on account of Hecate. Billycan decided not to bring it up.

As for the rest of Hecate's lavish garments, tapestries, and gold and silver finery, Billycan simply gave it all away. Never had he seen the Toscan rats so colorful. Children chased each other around the pillars, with vibrant silk scarves wrapped around their middles. Parents stored their coarse burlap cloaks, and now dressed in rich fabrics of dazzling colors.

Ajax took in the room. "You've done a good thing here. I

would have left the room locked up forever, if not for your coaxing, thinking the memories of Hecate were too painful for any of us. Time does heal all wounds, it seems."

Billycan chuckled as two little ones zipped by him, a blur of tails and color. "But your wounds are still raw. Eventually you would have done the same thing."

"I doubt that." Ajax snorted. "I'd be more likely to burn her things to ashes."

Thinking back to that night in the Catacombs when he burned down Clover's quarters, Billycan could sympathize with the wrath that burned inside Ajax. "But you didn't, did you? Even with all that she'd done, you didn't. There was a time when my need for revenge drove me to do horrible things. In that way, Hecate and I were very much alike, but you're better than that," said Billycan. "You are *good*."

"I suppose," Ajax replied. "Where did Hecate come from— originally, I mean? How did she come into your throng back in Trillium?"

"She was there well before Killdeer brought me into the fold. She was nothing more than a foot soldier back then, relatively insignificant. I took notice of her, though, watching as she quickly proved herself as vicious as an alley cat and shrewder than most of the males." Billycan snorted. "*I* was the one who promoted her to high major. I saw her promise." He glanced around the opulent room. "Had I let her be, perhaps none of this would have happened."

"Little by little, Hecate betrayed herself here in Tosca. Her stories became vaguer and vaguer, details blurred and changed. The more rats she recruited to her side, the more confident she felt, causing her to make mistakes. She began to show her true colors. Perhaps Hecate's self-control is waning again, and those closest to her in Nightshade are finally seeing the cracks in her façade."

Before Billycan could respond, a collective gasp filled the hall. Every rat stopped what it was doing and stared fixedly at the throne room's archway. Ajax leaped to his feet, astonished.

Silvius stood in the doorway, his coat washed and clean. Glancing around the room, Billycan saw tears rolling down many faces. Small ones pulled at their parents, asking who the tall white rat was, while the older ones' faces lit up, clearly remembering good King Silvius.

"I'm the only one who's seen him in years," whispered Ajax. "He looks just like he used to—a true king."

Silvius took in his subjects. A warm smile emerged, his red eyes twinkling against the white marble pillars. "No tears, now. I'm all right, my children," he said in a serene voice. He looked at Ajax. "In truth, this is the best I've felt in some time. Meeting Billycan, another rat imprisoned in that lab, made me realize something."

"What?" asked Ajax.

"That I need to do more."

"I'm so glad you came to see me. I don't get many visitors."

Duncan's eyes followed the steam from the teapot, which swirled in front of Mol's cage, causing the blue moth to jump excitedly. "It smells good," he said.

Elvi held out her paw, revealing dried pink petals. "I'll let you in on a little secret. This flower, it's what makes my tea taste so good. When I was in Tosca, I used it many times. My tea seems to soothe others."

Duncan stared at the flowers. "You brought them all the way from Tosca?"

"When I left Tosca, I could bring very few things." She

nodded around her chamber. "A few silk tapestries, some silver teacups. Everything else I had to leave behind. But these flowers, I knew they had to come with me." She smiled. "My tea brings joy, does it not?"

"Oh yes, everyone says it's the best tea in Nightshade City." Duncan made a sour face. "Much better than Clover's. Her tea is terrible."

"We can't be too critical, dear. We all have different gifts. Mine is making people happy with my tea." Her eyes narrowed as she filled Duncan's cup. "It brings me great joy. And soon, when you visit your brother, it will make me happier than you could ever imagine . . . the happiest of all."

Bostwick Hall was full of life. It had been a long time since Nightshade City had had an official party, and even though the timing was not the best given the unknown fate of the missing Hunters, the Council decided they would continue with the Naming Celebration, now an annual event celebrating their freedom and the night Nightshade City came to be.

Fall had swept in quickly, and dampened spirits needed to be lifted. Restless rats always felt the need to explore, and since Juniper had not yet put a ban on the citizens' comings and goings Topside, the well-timed celebration might quell their anxiety just enough to keep everyone underground, at least for a little while.

Vincent sat silently, watching. Rats rolled barrels of Carro ale past him. Cole's wife, Lali, had planned the menu. Plates of fine cheese and salted meats sat on every table. Steaming platters of smoked sausage and baskets piled high with Lali's famous bitonberry biscuits whizzed by him. It took him back to the first party Nightshade City ever had, the Naming Celebration. He remembered how different things were just four years ago. Though he'd tried to be brave for Victor's sake, he was scared stiff back then. Escaping the Catacombs, facing down Killdeer . . .

He looked proudly at Juniper. What could he say about him? Juniper had taken Vincent and Victor in, given them a place to live, and championed their father's memory. He gave them love, pure and simple. He'd been a father to them in every sense.

Vincent thought of his mother and father. He prayed that they would have approved of what he had done in his life—and what he was about to do.

He looked across the room at Clover. She was laughing and dancing, twirling in a chaotic circle with Texi and Oleander, as Carn, Suttor, and Victor danced around them. She looked stunning, with her fawn-colored fur and marigold eyes, and of course that beaming smile.

"Why don't you join us?" called Victor. "What are you doing over here all by your lonesome?" Catching his breath, he sat down next to his brother.

"Where's Petra?" asked Vincent.

"She'll be here soon. Her parents *still* won't let her see me unescorted, so she's coming with them. It's so unfair."

Vincent laughed. "Serves you right. You're always trying to convince her to sneak out!"

"True," said Victor, grinning mischievously, "but I'm quite worth sneaking out for." He raised an eyebrow. "You're lucky. Juniper lets you and Clover go out on your own anytime you like."

"We *are* older than you and Petra." He smiled in Clover's direction, keeping his eyes on her as he spoke.

Victor leaned in and stared craftily at his older brother, still transfixed by Clover. "What's got into you? You're acting strange tonight . . . all *sappy*. You *never* act like that, thank the Saints." Still watching Vincent, who seemed to be in some love-sick stupor, Victor suddenly gasped as though he'd just witnessed an appalling crime. He grabbed his brother's arm and punched it as hard as he could.

"Hey!" shouted Vincent. "What'd you do *that* for? That hurt!"

"Don't play dumb with me, Nightshade. After all, I *know* you! There's something you're not telling me."

Rubbing his arm, Vincent broke into an ear-to-ear grin. "I *couldn't* tell you. You know you can't keep a secret. You get that doltish smirk on your face—a dead giveaway! This time you *must* be quiet, please."

Victor looked at Clover. "I can't *believe* you didn't tell me!"

"Victor, please," said Vincent, "quiet down. I'm begging you. Only Juniper knows."

"Well," said Victor, motioning to Clover as she spun with Oleander and Texi in a dizzy circle, "when were you planning on asking her?"

"I've decided I'm not quite ready. It can keep. I'll ask her in due time."

Victor knew his brother too well. "Due time, my backside! If we do it your way, you'll have one foot in the grave before you work up the nerve." With that, Victor raced to the center of the room. Jumping up onto the makeshift stage where the band was playing, he stomped his foot and slapped his tail against the wood. "Excuse me!" he shouted as loud as he could. "I beg your pardon, one and all, but I've something to say!" The par-tygoers settled down a bit, but not to his liking. "I said, *excuse me*. Now hush up!" Finally Bostwick Hall quieted. All eyes were on him. He glanced over at Vincent, who sat on his stool trying unsuccessfully to hide his face in his paws. "I've an announce-ment to make—and it's a whopper."

Juniper glanced at Vincent's mortified face and then at Victor. "Victor," he called out in his most serious tone, "what are you up to?"

Giving an unbearably obnoxious smile, Victor winked at his brother. "I'm up to no good, Juniper. *That's* what I'm up to." The crowd laughed.

"I see," said Juniper, walking toward Vincent. "And what, young Victor, do you have to announce?"

"I might as well die right now," said Vincent, wishing the floor would open up and swallow him whole.

Juniper chuckled. "Son," he whispered, "we've all been waiting for this moment—Victor the longest. You've no idea how many times he's asked me about the two of you. He loves you both. Clover is as much his sister as you are his brother. Just as Clover needs to hear the words, so does he."

Vincent got to his feet. He approached the stage, holding his paw out to his brother, who gladly pulled him up. Vincent stared out at the crowd. He saw all his friends. Oleander and Carn held paws, waiting excitedly. Cole gave Suttor a fatherly shove and the two of them laughed quietly. Ulrich stood happily next to Texi, while Virden and Ragan just smiled.

Clover stood in front of the stage, looking up at Vincent confusedly. He jumped back down from the stage right in front of her and took her paw in his, holding it to his chest. There were so many things he wanted to say, but at that moment none of it came to mind except one thing. "The day I met you, I knew that you were special—and not because our fathers were best friends. You were a survivor. You stayed strong and lived through Killdeer's reign, but you never lost sight of who you were, always with your sunny outlook. After all you've been through, you have the most open, compassionate, tender heart anyone could ever know."

Clover's pulse raced. She looked at Juniper, who smiled at her, wrapping his arm around Mother Gallo's shoulder. "It's all right, dear," Mother Gallo whispered to her. Julius, Nomi, and the other children gathered around her. "Your heart will lead you."

"Say yes, Clover!" cried Julius. "You must say yes!"

"Shhh," said Juniper in a hushed voice, holding a claw to his lips. "That part hasn't happened yet."

"Say yes!" repeated Nomi, bouncing up and down.

Mother Gallo scooped her daughter up in her arms. "Hush, dear."

Vincent looked at Clover's expectant face, the face he had first seen four years ago when he'd reached his arms up to help her into the tunnel they'd dug to Nightshade City. "Say yes . . . to *me*." She looked around nervously. "Marry me, Clover."

"Oh!" said Clover, her legs weakening. Trying to block out the noise of the crowd, she closed her eyes, recalling the look on Vincent's face the first time she ever saw him, his determined green eyes. Clover's feet suddenly felt rock solid. Her thundering heart wasn't fearful. It was joyful. She took a step

toward Vincent. She reached out, holding his face in both her paws. "You mean *everything* to me. You are my family." She hugged him.

After a moment, Vincent pulled back and looked at her. "Is—is that a *yes*, then?"

Clover nodded. "Yes." She turned around and looked at the breathless crowd. "Yes!" she shouted. She turned back to Vincent. Through the cheers, laughter, and singing, all she could see was him.

Vincent closed his eyes and held her close, lost in the lemony scent of her fur.

"Silvius," whispered Ajax, after the long line of Toscans had greeted their king at a spur-of-the-moment celebration feast, "are you *really* all right?"

Silvius looked around the hall at all the smiling faces. "I'm certainly not cured . . . but I feel *better*, more like my old self." He rested his chin on his paw. "Hearing Billycan's story brought something back in me, something I've not felt in ages."

"And what's that?" asked Ajax curiously.

"Determination to stop Hecate," said Silvius, "to never let another rat go through what we went through." He huffed crossly. "It's never right to let a single soul control the fates of so many others. Before Hecate, we worked together, as a kingdom. You were my adviser and friend, as were many others. Decisions were not made unilaterally by me; they were made by all."

"You were—and are—a good king."

"I never wanted to be king," said Silvius. "I never asked for that. I only wanted to make lives better."

Ajax smiled, looking around the bustling hall. "Then you accomplished your goal, despite Hecate. We only called you king because you deserved it."

"Ajax," said Silvius, "I cannot lead our kingdom anymore. At the moment I feel quite lucid, but I fear it will not last. You *must* lead these rats. I will counsel you whenever I can. You are like a son to me. Back in that dreadful lab, the humans bred us most unnaturally, taking bits and pieces of us with their diabolical needles and injecting the poor would-be mothers of our future children. It was unspeakable. I never knew who my children were, or their mother. That is a heartache that will never leave me."

Cocking his head, Billycan reached out and grabbed Silvius by the wrist. "Did you know a female named Lenore?" he asked urgently. "She was my mother. Did you know *her*?"

Silvius exhaled. "The lab was very much segregated. The females were kept far away from us males and the children. I'm sorry, my boy," he said, seeing the hope in Billycan's face. "I did not know her." He smiled weakly, patting Billycan's paw. "Though I wish I had."

Billycan bowed his head and closed his eyes. He laughed softly. With this new way of being, this new life, came much suffering. In some ways he wished he had his callousness back. When nothing mattered but getting what he wanted, life was less painful.

"Ajax, you must take the reins of this kingdom right now," declared Silvius. Ajax's jaw dropped, his black skin turning a pasty gray. "You can do this, lad. You must."

"But why now?" asked Ajax.

"Because Billycan leaves the island tonight," Silvius replied. "I'm certainly old." He laughed. "I may even be crazy, but the stakes are too high for us not to do *something*. We must at least try to warn the rats of Nightshade, unless they've already come to a bitter end."

CHAPTER SIX

Fear

WIPING SWEATY PAWS ON HIS COAT, Duncan nervously wheeled around a corner. He looked down the dim corridor and listened. The only sounds he could hear were indistinct whispers coming from behind the large metal door of the prison corridor.

Heart pounding, Duncan looked through the barred window of the door and knocked. A moment later his brother arrived.

Suttor smiled. "Duncan," he said cheerfully. "What are you doing here?"

"Well," said Duncan, "I just thought I'd stop by and say hello. We never seem to see each other anymore. I brought you some tea."

"Thanks!" said Suttor, surprised and pleased. He scratched his head. "But you hate this place."

Duncan looked around nervously. "I—I just don't like it here. It's a bit creepy."

"Kar dislikes it even more than you," said Suttor. "At least you two get to work with Lali in Bostwick kitchen, though I'd hate all that cleaning up after dinner. I'll take creepy over cleaning anytime. Besides, it's not so bad down here, gives me time to read and to think, a little peace and quiet . . . when the prisoners aren't grousing, that is."

Through the small barred window, Duncan looked down the corridor. "Aren't there any other guards?"

"Don't worry. The doors are bolted tight," Suttor replied, "made of the thickest ironwood. Even the cells are lined with it, so the prisoners can't dig their way out." He nodded to a cell door. "Each prisoner has a small window for food, just the perfect size for a single dinner plate, no more." A rat cursed from inside his cell. Suttor grinned. "The old Kill Army majors can whine and complain all they please, start a right fuss if they like. They'll never get out." He snickered, then lowering his voice, said, "Even old High Major Foiber, he's the one always swearing, but I'd swear too if I had that frightful hairless skin."

"Juniper seems to have thought of everything," said Duncan, his confidence growing. "What would you do, though, if one of the prisoners took ill? Some of the majors are getting on in years, especially High Majors Schnauss and Foiber. How can you help them if they're all locked up?"

Suttor snorted. "What do you care about those old codgers? Rats like them tend to live forever! No rest for the wicked." He leaned in to the tiny window. "There's a metal cabinet right here next to the door." He rapped on it with his paw, causing it to clang. "You can't see it from out there, but it contains the cell keys." He laughed. "But even that's locked up tight!"

"And who holds the key to *that*?"

"Why, I do, of course," said Suttor, feeling the leather cord around his neck that held the iron key, partially hidden by his spotted coat. "How else would I get to a prisoner if one suddenly took ill? I've had this key around my neck since I can remember, and you've never known what it's for?"

"Well, what if the prisoner's faking—a ruse to escape? You could get hurt . . . or worse."

Suttor laughed at that. "Little brother, you've thought about this a lot, haven't you? Any prisoner who gets to go out for any reason would be shackled before a guard unlocked his door."

"But what if they're sick and moaning on the ground? How can you shackle them?"

"The Council Chamber is not far from here. We've been instructed to fetch a Council member for backup if that situation ever arises."

"Has it ever happened before?"

"Old Foiber pretended to be sick once. He groaned on the ground, clutching his stomach, putting up a right fuss. When he wouldn't crawl over to the bars so I could shackle him, I *knew* he was faking."

"What happened?"

"I laughed at him!" said Suttor. "He started his normal screaming and cursing, jumping to his feet, shaking his fists at me." He shook his head. "It was a comical scene."

"I'm glad I came to see you," said Duncan. He inwardly laughed. All this time he'd been so frightened of the prison corridor. "When is your next shift?"

"Day after tomorrow," said Suttor.

"Can I come back then? I'll bring more tea."

Suttor smiled shrewdly at his brother. "Do you think you could smuggle in a basket of Lali's bitonberry biscuits, too?"

"Consider it done," said Duncan.

Reaching through the bars, Suttor cuffed his brother's

shoulder playfully. "You're a good brother, Duncan. Me, you, and Kar, we've made it through thick and thin. The three of us have seen it all, and we survived."

Duncan smiled contentedly. He was proud of himself. He'd faced down a longtime fear. He couldn't wait to thank Elvi. She'd changed his life.

Billycan was tense. The journey back from Tosca had taken far longer than expected. The boat he had stowed away on had made countless stops at various islands that dotted the Hellgate Sea, picking up exotic goods to sell in Trillium. He was glad to be off the boat and away from the acrid smell of water-chip root, Tosca's only export. He'd hidden in a crate of it on the journey, and the putrid stench was overwhelming.

Hidden by the darkness of the early morning, Billycan watched for what felt like hours as rat after rat darted up and down the pier, attending to their duties.

The dock rats were a rough sort. They contended with the humans every day, easily outwitting them. In his dark days, Billycan had once tried to take over their operation. Had the Bloody Coup not happened when it did, he might have succeeded.

Billycan's head was pounding, throbbing in time with his rapidly beating heart. He pulled at his ears, listening intently even through the pain. He remained silent in the alley, looking, listening, waiting, which was beginning to drive him mad. He didn't like to wait.

Suddenly a huge rat approached from behind. Billycan turned to face him. He was a big, brown fellow. One ear was all but gone and the other had a rather sizable bite out of it. His fur was disheveled and missing in a few places, revealing deep battle scars. His tail was mangled, and looked more like a frayed piece of twine than a proper rat's tail. The rat was battle-worn, thought Billycan.

"You don't belong here!" said the rat in a gruff voice. "You're in my territory. What do you want?" He flared his long claws. He gave Billycan a wicked sneer, grunting arrogantly. The rat's rancor poured off of him like the stench of rotting meat.

Billycan circled swiftly around the rat, his body shaking with suppressed rage.

"Well?" demanded the rat.

"I'm waiting for someone," said Billycan. "Moreover, this is the dock rats' territory, not yours."

"Is that so?" The rat grinned crookedly, flexing his digits. He cracked his neck from side to side, a sure sign he was preparing for a fight.

Billycan was in no mood to trifle with this rat. He shook his head resignedly. "We are not going to settle this amicably, are we?"

The rat grinned deviously. "Well, now, where would be the fun in that?"

Billycan's eyes narrowed to dark slits. His voice dropped to a callous whisper. "Do yourself a favor, as you don't look like the brightest of fellows. Do not challenge me. You'll lose."

"I'll kill you!" shouted the rat, now thoroughly infuriated.

Billycan sighed. "I'll say it again, slowly this time, so you understand me. You'll lose."

The rat snorted disdainfully. Flaring his teeth and growling, he immediately circled in closer. He inspected Billycan, eyeing him for a soft spot.

Billycan noted the rat's snout. It was oversized, just as he was—its underside slightly bulbous and rounded. His meaty chest had several deep scars on it. He'd been injured there before. And then there were his eyes, bulging like swollen black globes. A plan formed in Billycan's head: snout, chest, eyes, and finally jaw, in that order—four steps.

Still circling, the rat suddenly took a deft turn, charging at breakneck speed. Here was Billycan's chance. Instead of jumping to the left or right, he dived underneath him, causing him to topple backwards as Billycan struck the bottom of the rat's snout with his head. The rat groaned loudly in agony. Step one—complete.

"Lucky shot, is all," said the rat as he staggered to his feet. He wiped blood from his mouth, stumbling dizzily to the right and then back to the left, clearly unable to focus, his brain ringing from the blow.

Quickly now, thought Billycan, time for step two. Using his heavy tail as a whip, Billycan came up from behind, cuffing the rat hard in the chest—the blow so powerful Billycan's tail smarted. The rat coughed and groaned, a fine mist of blood flying from his mouth.

Billycan laughed gleefully, circling tightly around the rat, who teetered, unable to stand straight any longer. Billycan threw himself to the left and then quickly back to the right, hurling himself into the rat's cranium, striking with such force Billycan could feel the bone around the rat's eye break. Step three—achieved.

His once rigid body now slack, the rat moaned feebly, bobbing back and forth. Billycan came at him one final time. Charging him head on, Billycan lunged at implausible speed, his arm lurching forward, grabbing the rat's lower jaw. He locked on to his mandible, pulling downward. The rat howled as his jaw cracked. Billycan's body shivered with delight.

Step four—accomplished.

Task—concluded.

The rat fell to the ground with a heavy thud. Billycan was mesmerized by the sight. He surveyed the damage. Blood trickled from the rat's mouth, eye, and chest, his eye socket crushed, his jaw nearly detached, undoubtedly fractured. The rat would be lucky if he kept his sight in the wounded eye, but Billycan suspected he'd probably lose it.

All and all, recovery would take at least three months. The healing of the rat's ego, on the other hand, might take far longer.

Billycan's agonizing headache had vanished. He looked around, unsure where he was. He looked down at his bloodied paws, uncertain how the fight he wound up in even started.

The rat was out cold on the pavement. Billycan sat down next to him, confused, but it seemed as if a fog had suddenly been lifted. He lay on his back and looked up at the stars, their light dimmed by the illuminated city.

He was glad to be home.

"Oh, Clover," said Mother Gallo, digging through her chest of sewing supplies, "this is all so exciting—a wedding!" At her feet Nomi squealed with delight, covering herself in strands of beads and ribbons that had fallen to the floor. "Only a few days until the big event. There is so much to do in so little time." She paced around the fire pit, tapping her chin. "Why, there's your sash—I'm thinking a lovely yellow to match your eyes— the invitations, the decor, the seating, the menu, the music, and so many other details. I almost don't know where to begin."

"Really, I'm fine with a small, quiet ceremony," replied Clover, seeing the worry on Mother Gallo's face. "There's no need for you or Uncle to fuss. After four years, Vincent and I don't want to wait any longer than necessary."

"If anyone knows how you feel, it's me," said Mother Gallo,

thinking back on how long she was apart from Juniper. "You and Vincent are right. Don't wait! And about having a small, quiet ceremony, well, you can simply forget about that. Nightshade City will have the wedding of the century!"

"Of the century!" repeated Nomi as she placed a large pink bow atop her head.

Clover giggled. She crouched down, helping Nomi put another necklace over her head. "I suppose it's settled, then. Thank you for your help." She paused for a moment, remembering their first meeting in the Catacombs and how Mother Gallo had safely delivered her to her uncle. "Thank you . . . for *everything*. Without you, I doubt there'd be any wedding celebration for me. I owe my life to you."

"My dear," said Mother Gallo, ceasing her harried pacing. She smiled down at Nomi. "You are just as much a daughter to me as this one. And though I could never take her place, it's my pleasure—more so, my *honor*—to fill in for your mother on occasions such as these." She held an anxious paw to her heart. "I only hope I do her proud."

"Mother Gallo, you already have."

Billycan had moved away from the injured brown rat, down the pier, where he hid behind a pile of ropes. Finally the rat Billycan had been waiting for emerged from the dark. Its coat was a gleaming cinnamon. Its eyes shone a brilliant violet, reflecting the cold water.

Billycan wasted no time. "Gwenfor!" he called out, trying to keep his voice down. The rat turned her head in his direction. "Over here!"

Long and imperial, the rat stood stiffly on her haunches. "Who's there?" she asked, baring her lethal teeth. "Who calls me?"

Stepping into a thin shaft of light, Billycan showed himself. He stared at her. "*I* do."

Gwenfor stood her ground, looking at him coolly. "Billycan, we had an agreement, you and I. Why then have you come? What is the meaning of this intrusion?"

"You *owe* me," said Billycan decisively. "It's high time I collected payment."

"I owe you nothing," she said, her regal mouth slipping into a sneer. "You gave me your word you'd never come for me. My debt is paid. I *never* should have trusted you."

"You're quite right," he replied grimly. "You never should have trusted me, but things have changed. Many lives hang in the balance, possibly your own. That being the case, our little arrangement is null and void."

"What are you talking about? Apart from your own skin, since when do you care about lives hanging in the balance?"

"I've no doubt you haven't forgotten Killdeer, his plans for you and your rats."

Her eyes flooding with hatred, Gwenfor spat bitterly on the pier. "How could I forget? We celebrated for days upon word of his death." She took a step forward, trying to get a better look at him. "What's different about you?" she asked, cocking her head curiously. "Your voice, it's . . . calmer. And your eyes, they are not the same."

Billycan ignored her observations. "A rat from Killdeer's reign has returned—one who wielded much power, but even more venom. She and members of her throng have infiltrated Nightshade. There will be bloodshed."

"Who?" demanded Gwenfor.

"Hecate," he said coolly.

"But—but why?"

"To take power, of course, to reclaim the throne in Killdeer's name—to kill any rat she feels has wronged her, from the most powerful rat in all of Nightshade down to the most innocent child. She is out for blood."

"Elvi, what possible objection could you have to Texi being in the wedding?" asked Juniper. "She's one of Clover's dearest friends."

"After what Texi *did* I do not think you should reward her in such a way," Elvi replied with conviction. "She hasn't been able to concentrate on her studies since Clover asked her, dizzy with thoughts of dancing and merriment. How is she to pay for her crimes, if we indulge such folly?" She shook her head. "It's utterly ridiculous."

"Her *crimes*?" said Juniper, incensed by the choice of word. He got up brusquely from his chair. "What Texi did, she only did to gain acceptance from her sisters—to feel loved. She thought she was doing the right thing, and in the end she protected Julius from them. Her heart has *always* been in the right place, and there is no crime in that!" He exhaled, not wanting to broach his mounting concerns with Elvi, but it was time. He lowered his voice. "Why must you be so hard on her? Of late you have *not* been yourself. You seem so angry, dare I say bitter, not the Elvi I know so well, not the one I grew up with in the Catacombs." He rubbed his brow. "We've all noticed it. There's been talk among the Council. It's clear to everyone. Many of the Council members have grown wary of you, afraid to speak their minds in your presence lest you explode." He reclaimed his seat. "After the harsh life you endured in Tosca and all that happened last year, I'd think you'd be happy to have some peace, but you only stew with rage."

Getting up from her chair, Elvi fetched her teapot. She turned her back to Juniper, her mouth curling into a sneer. "I know I've been . . . cold lately." She sighed. "Happiness is an elusive thing for a rat such as me. Every moment of joy I've ever felt has been stolen. Perhaps my heart has been stolen as well."

"Elvi, I had no idea how deeply you'd been wounded," said Juniper, watching her small, cloaked frame curl over her teapot. "You've always been so self-assured. I suppose it never occurred to me that your scars from the past could run so deep . . . and for that I am sorry. As for your stolen heart, I'm afraid it's still very much with you. In fact, you've a bigger heart than any rat I know. Texi is proof of that. You've built up her confidence, and we are all grateful for that, but just as you've built her up, I've noticed she's become rather dependent on you. It seems she can't even breathe these days without asking your permission first. She needs to make up her own mind, make her *own* decisions."

Turning around with the sweetest of smiles, Elvi cocked her head. "You always put things into perspective, Juniper. Here I thought it was good for her, but perhaps I *have* been a bit iron-handed. I only thought I was helping her."

"You *have* helped her," said Juniper, "but it's high time she stood on her own two feet."

"Agreed," she said, reaching for two teacups in her small cupboard. "Standing next to Clover will be a special reward for Texi. She has earned it."

"You've earned it as well," said Juniper. "Without you as a teacher, Texi could not be the self-assured rat she is today. Elvi, you should be proud. You deserve it."

She grinned broadly. "You're right. I *do* deserve it." She set a teacup in front of Juniper.

"Oh, no, thank you," said Juniper, holding up his paw. "I must admit I feel more energized lately, more lucid. Probably just happenstance, but it all started when I stopped drinking tea." He chuckled. "I know it sounds foolish, but for that reason alone I'll politely pass."

Taking the teacup, Elvi slowly turned back to the cupboard, concealing her resentment in a taut grin. She gritted her teeth as she spoke. "Where, then, does Maddy see our Texi standing in the wedding party?" she asked stiffly.

"Well, Clover asked her to be the maid of honor, and though I don't know much about these affairs, I suppose Texi will stand beside the happy couple."

With much effort, Elvi controlled her shaky breath and trembling paws as she replaced the teacup in her cupboard. The anticipation was almost too much to bear. Time was drawing near. Soon everyone in Nightshade would know the name of Hecate.

CHAPTER SEVEN
Payback

THE BELANCORT QUARTERS BUSTLED with energy. Mother Gallo whirled around Clover, checking and double-checking every inch of her perfectly pressed yellow silk sash. Mother Gallo's older sons were supposed to be keeping Julius and Nomi calm, but their own excitement only led to more bedlam. Hob, Tuk, and Gage dashed about the quarters, chasing Texi, Julius, and Nomi, who screamed in blissful terror each time one of them reached for their tails.

Juniper walked up behind Clover as she regarded herself in the mirror. He rested his paws on her shoulders. "You look stunning, my dear." He sighed. "But are you certain you're ready for this? You don't *have* to get married, you know. Vincent will wait."

"I've never been more certain of anything in my life," she said decisively. She laughed, smiling at her uncle in the mirror's reflection. "Besides, you love Vincent."

"Yes, that's true," agreed Juniper, "but aren't all doting

fathers expected to try to talk their daughters out of marriage just before they walk down the aisle?"

"I suppose so," said Clover.

"Barcus would love Vincent too, but knowing my brother, it's exactly what he'd say to you if he were here."

Clover glanced up. "I've a feeling he is here . . . and mother and my brothers. I can feel them all around us."

"So can I," said Juniper, giving her shoulders an encouraging squeeze.

Clutching a needle and thread for last-minute mending, Mother Gallo rushed up beside her husband. "Now Juniper, you aren't expecting to wear that mucky cloak and ragged old satchel to the wedding, are you? Why, you look like a vagrant! Please, for Clover's sake, take them off."

Chuckling, Juniper kissed the top of his wife's head. "Anything for you, dear." He reached for his leather bag, about to take it off.

Clover spun around. "No, Uncle," she said firmly. "Stay just the way you are."

"Oh dear," said Mother Gallo, aghast. "You don't want your uncle dressed like this at your wedding, Clover."

"Actually . . . I do," she replied. "It's who he is. I've never known him to look another way. I want the same uncle who rescued me from the Catacombs to be at my wedding." She giggled. "Not some dapper imposter."

"Very well," said Mother Gallo, throwing her paws in the air. "It's your wedding, and if you want to be given away by this grimy excuse for a rat, then so be it." She straightened the collar of Juniper's cloak. "I suppose it will have to do." Try as she might, she couldn't help but smile. "He's still quite handsome, this one, muck and all."

"I'll take that as a compliment," said Juniper with a wink.

"Now then, I'm off to petrify the groom about the many pitfalls of matrimony, starting with his lovely wife harping on his appearance for the rest of his pitiful life."

"Oh you," said Mother Gallo, swatting his arm.

Juniper looked around at the frenzied activity. "I daresay you'll have no objection to one less rat in the house."

"Goodness no," said Mother Gallo as Julius and Texi whizzed by her, "and please, take the boys with you." Nomi squealed as Tuk and Hob snatched at her tail. "It's absolute madness in here!"

"It *is* madness," agreed Clover as she took in the chaos, thinking back to her many silent, solitary days trapped in the Catacombs, "but the very best kind."

The carts and vendors of Nightshade's city square had vanished, and in their place were long vines interwoven with honeysuckle and purple saxifrage, hanging from the grand rotunda. The white and purple flowers thrived in Trillium's chilly climate, and Mother Gallo thought they were a perfect testament to Vincent and Clover's endurance through the many trials of their young lives.

Nightshade citizens had funneled in from the corridors, each resident gasping at the transformed city square, a hanging forest of white and purple, its sweet perfume winding through the ordinarily musty underground city.

Vincent sat next to his brother on the steps leading up to the makeshift altar. "Maybe this was a bad idea," he said to Victor, furrowing his brow. "I think we should have waited. The Hunter rats are still missing, and here we are having a wedding, *my* wedding. Somehow it gives me an ill feeling I can't seem to shake."

"Cheer up," said Victor sharply. "For Saints' sake, it's your *wedding* day. The citizens *need* a distraction, and so do you. You've always been a worrywart, you know." Vincent opened his mouth to reply. "And before you say it, I realize you've had your reasons to be worried. You had to raise me, for one.

"What I'm trying to say is you *deserve* a little happiness. For once in your life it's all right to be selfish, brother. No one will fault you for it. You've *earned* it."

"For the record, I'm *not* a worrywart"—Vincent playfully punched Victor's shoulder—"but you *are* a good brother. You're relentlessly annoying, but you're a good brother all the same."

"Practically the whole city's here," said Victor. The front rows had filled up with close friends, family, and the Council. He saw Hob, Mother Gallo's youngest, sitting next to Kar. Kar looked around the room as though trying to spot someone. Victor's forehead wrinkled. "Speaking of good brothers, where are Suttor and Duncan? Kar's looking a little lost, sitting there next to two empty chairs."

Using two upside-down buckets and a small wooden crate, Suttor and Duncan had set up a makeshift table and chairs in the prison corridor.

Even with some of the prisoners commenting and complaining in the background, Duncan felt at ease. He had Elvi to thank for that. She'd released him from his fear and made him realize just how silly he'd been all this time. It gave him high hopes for the future, when they would navigate the museum with him leading the way.

Suttor talked with his mouth full, already on his second biscuit. "Your timing is so good," he said in a muddled voice. He finally swallowed his bite. "I'm starving!"

Duncan poured them each some tea. "When do you get to leave for the wedding?"

"My replacement should be here soon. I'm glad we get to eat before the ceremony. They always seem to drag on, and by the time it's over I'm famished."

"Me too," said Duncan, pushing a cup of tea in front of Suttor.

"Here," said Suttor, pointing to the basket of biscuits. "Take another before I eat them all." He picked up his cup and drained it. "Ah . . . that's better."

Duncan laughed. "Slow down," he said. "You're going to make yourself sick."

"Lali's biscuits and Elvi's tea," said Suttor. "If I'm going to get sick over something, it might as well be the two things I love!" He exhaled contentedly. "Pour me another cup, will you?"

As Duncan picked up the teapot, Suttor put a paw to his forehead and rubbed it. "You all right?" Duncan asked.

"I think so," said Suttor. "You're right, though, maybe I shouldn't overdo it. I feel . . . a little funny." He began to sway slightly on his stool. "I . . . I . . ."

"Suttor?"

Suttor dropped to a heap on the dirt floor.

Falling to his knees, Duncan grabbed his brother by the shoulders, gently shaking him. "Suttor, wake up!" He put his ear to Suttor's chest, but all he could hear was the dizzying rush of blood going to his head as panic struck him.

The prisoners began to shout and curse. They banged impatient fists against the bars and scratched their doors with eager claws.

"That's it, boy!" called out a voice that Duncan quickly recognized as High Major Foiber's. "Be loyal to your High Ministry!"

There was a banging on the outer door. Duncan gasped. A gray rat with yellow eyes stuck his snout in between the bars of the small window. "What's going on in there? Let me in straightaway!"

"My brother!" shouted Duncan. "Something's happened to him. He's passed out on the floor. Please, help me!" He ripped the leather cord off of Suttor's neck and raced for the door, fumbling with the key. "I don't know what happened. He was fine just a minute ago!"

The rat pushed his way past Duncan. He crouched over Suttor and patted his face. "Yep, he's out like a light. Good work!"

"Good work?" said Duncan, horrified by the comment.

The rat laughed riotously. "Stupid oaf! I'm amazed you pulled it off. Now go, before I release these cutthroats upon you!"

"What—what are you talking about?" demanded Duncan. He looked vacantly around at the growling prisoners. "Re . . . release them?"

The rat rolled his eyes wearily. "Never have I encountered such a mealy-mouthed, slack-jawed rat. And look at you; you're built like a mountain! What a waste. Now go!"

"You—you want me to leave? What about Suttor?"

The rat stood upright, nudging a motionless Suttor with his foot. "Hecate was right," said the rat. "'You'll see,' she told me, 'I'll pull on his oversized heartstrings and the big orange one will do whatever I say.'" He laughed some more. "Oh, positively priceless!"

"Who's Hecate?"

"You really are stupid, aren't you?" asked the rat. "Hecate is Elvi. Your beloved little Elvi, the rat Juniper and the others knew from the old days, is long since dead—killed years ago when we were all forced onto that abysmal ship during the Great Flood. No one realized we were fighting for the other side—we were the enemy! Well, they soon learned! Hecate is small and gray, just like that sugary Elvi was. I was glad the day we got rid of her, with her constant cheeriness." He snickered. "They matched even down to their black eyes, they did. After we returned, the scorching Toscan sun was the perfect excuse for any changes in poor little Elvi's appearance."

"I—I don't understand!"

"Of course you don't, you soft-headed lump. Elvi *is* Hecate—they are one and the same." He pointed to the growling majors. "And this handsome lot, they're with me."

"But I thought you were the guard—my brother's relief so he could go to the wedding."

"Oh yes, the guard. That chap's going to have quite a headache when he wakes up—if he does at all. I made sure of that." The rat vanished out the main door as he spoke, quickly returning with a large burlap sack. He dumped it on the ground, lethal weapons scattering everywhere. "You, young rat, have brought back the High Ministry—*Killdeer's* High Ministry. If you weren't so dense, I might bloody well thank you."

Duncan began to shake uncontrollably. "The—the High Ministry? Killdeer?"

"You're looking at one of his lost majors—one who never had a chance to enjoy the easy life in the Catacombs. Me and my boys spent a decade on that wretched island with Hecate, biding our time. Now we're back to reclaim what is rightfully ours." He shouted at the prisoners, who cursed and snarled from their cells. "Ready, lads? We've been waiting a long time for this!"

"Hurry, Major Ragwort!" Foiber called out. "I can't take another moment in here!"

"Yes!" added Schnauss. "Just let me at Juniper and his precious Council. I will rip them limb from filthy Loyalist limb!"

Ragwort wasted no more time. He unlocked the metal box

that held the keys to the cells, and snatched as many as he could in his claws. He leered menacingly at Duncan. "If I was you, lad, I'd *run.*"

The citizens murmured, all growing impatient as time ticked by. "We'll have to start without them," whispered Juniper, glancing at the wedding official, who twitched his whiskers impatiently, rocking on his heels and huffing as he waited to begin the ceremony. "The guard relieving Suttor is probably running late. He and Duncan will be here soon, I'm sure."

"But Suttor is one of my closet friends," said Vincent, about to take his place at the altar. "I don't want to start without him."

"I know, son, but these things happen. Suttor will understand. Lali has piles of food ready and waiting for the reception. She'll have all our heads if it gets cold." He reached up and touched a purple flower dangling just above his head. "And Maddy will give us both twenty lashes if we leave these flowers to wilt any longer. Besides, single lads are more concerned with the festivities *after* the nuptials." He winked. "It's the celebration that's special to them, dancing with a pretty girl or two."

"I guess you're right," said Vincent.

"Good lad. No more time to waste." Vincent took the last step up to the altar, Victor taking his place by his side. Juniper nodded at the official. "We're ready."

Duncan barreled down the corridors, his heart feeling as if it might rip apart in his chest. He could hear the Kill Army majors thundering behind him. He turned the corner, dashing down the last corridor that led to the city square, the wedding official's raspy voice echoing through the rotunda.

He saw a sea of seated citizens in the distance, Clover

and Vincent above them at the altar, giving him the faintest glimmer of hope that maybe there was still time to stop this.

Gasping desperately for breath, Duncan called out, "Juniper! Cole! The—the prisoners, they're loose! Elvi is—" He heard a loud crack that resounded through his head, his voice losing all power. His whole body launched forward, striking the ground. He couldn't talk or take in air. As he stared at the ceiling of the corridor, a long gray form took shape above him. It was the rat with the yellow eyes.

The rat poked him with a long wooden cudgel. "I do applaud you for trying. You've got more pluck than I thought. Too late, though, lad . . . you're done for." The rat lifted the cudgel over Duncan's head.

Juniper glanced around the city square. Still no sign of Suttor or his brother. There was no reason for concern, but still it was odd. Suttor was never late. Juniper's ears perked, and his gaze stopped on one of the corridors. He heard a noise that sounded like shouting. He listened intently for a moment. Whatever it was, it was gone. He shook his head and turned back to Clover and Vincent at the altar.

Mother Gallo leaned in close to him. "Everything all right, dear?"

"Yes," he whispered, patting her paw. He regarded his niece. "She looks beautiful, doesn't she?"

"Our maid of honor, too," added Mother Gallo, watching Texi smile proudly as she stood at the altar across from Victor, the best man.

The official continued. "Vincent Nightshade, what say you? Do you wish Clover by your side, through good and ghastly, dark and daylight—two rats who build a bond, furthering our kind?"

"I . . . wish it," said Vincent shakily, more nervous now than he'd ever been even in the most perilous of circumstances. Victor snickered, causing Carn to do the same.

"And do you, Clover Belancort, wish Vincent by your side, through glee and grief, dawn and demise—two rats who build a bond, furthering our kind?"

Clover paused a small moment, taking everything in. She wanted to always remember Vincent's face, her family and friends, the city square—everything—just like it was at this very moment. She took a satisfied breath, then all the hairs on her body suddenly stood on end. A shiver shot up her back as a vaguely familiar sound flooded her ears. "I—" She couldn't make it out at first, but then it was quite clear. She remembered it from four years ago in the Catacombs, the night Vincent and Juniper helped her make her escape—the sound of pounding footsteps, vibrating through the corridors, coming for her. She looked at Vincent. "Do . . . do you hear that?"

He nodded and glanced uneasily around the square. Vincent's gaze fell upon Elvi in the second row. For some reason she'd stood up. Excusing herself politely, she made her way to the center aisle, and as she did so, rat after male rat stood up from the crowd of seated citizens. Vincent recognized many of them; various rats who lived in Nightshade, no one he knew in particular—the types who kept low profiles.

Still seated, Juniper looked up at her from his seat. "Elvi," he whispered, "what are you doing?"

Silently Elvi nodded at the standing rats. From their hiding places in cloaks, under chairs, ensnared in the flowers, weapon after weapon materialized in the paws of the rats. And these weren't just *any* weapons. Steel swords, hunting knives, battle-axes, and etched silver daggers just like the one Elvi carried— which she quickly revealed to the murmuring crowd and held up to Juniper's neck, forcing him to his feet. "I just sharpened it," she said, "so don't try anything."

Several armed rats swarmed the front rows, warning the Council and any other rat who might dare come to Juniper's aid to stay put.

"Elvi," said Mother Gallo, focusing on the dagger at her husband's throat, "what's the meaning of this?"

Elvi ripped off her black cloak, revealing her full form, something she hadn't done since returning from Tosca.

Even with the dagger aimed at him, Juniper slowly took a step back. A dark patch near Elvi's gray stomach traveled around her back, drenching nearly half of her in solid black.

Citizens took to their feet—and not just any citizens, but those who had been part of Killdeer's army, found innocent of wrongdoing by Nightshade's security. One such rat, a former major, jumped to his feet, looking as though he might be ill. "He-Hecate," he called out in a strangled voice, searching the crowd for other former majors. "She's *alive!*" One of Hecate's rats quickly pounced on him, knocking him out cold with the hilt of his sword.

Texi looked on in confusion. "Elvi?"

Smiling pleasantly, Hecate looked up at her on the altar and hurled a dagger in her direction. Texi caught it instinctively. "My name is Hecate." Her Toscan accent had evaporated. "High Major Hecate."

"You're . . . you're not Elvi?" Texi's eyes widened in horror. "You *lied*?"

"Yes, my dear. I *had* to. I was part of your great brother's army. You were too young to remember me. All this time, I've been waiting to reclaim what was his—to bring back the High Ministry to its former glory, to pick up where he left off."

"Why . . . why would you want to do that?" asked Texi, tears trickling down her cheeks. "My brother was not a good rat. He was bad. You said so yourself!"

"I had to say such things, but dearest girl, Killdeer was a good rat," said Hecate, keeping her eyes and dagger trained on Juniper. "Killdeer allowed me to prove myself, to show my strength, when no one else would. Without his teachings, I never would have survived in Tosca, biding my time until I could return to take back what he so unfairly lost."

Clover's face fell in misery. She'd been so defensive of Elvi, never allowing Vincent to speak ill of her when they were searching for the traitor last year. She looked at Vincent. "You were right all along."

He took her paw. "I never wanted to be."

"All the signs were right in front of me, all this time," said Juniper. "You've been acting so strange these past months, so very different from the sweet little girl I knew from the Catacombs." He looked regretfully at his citizens. "I'm such a fool."

Hecate laughed. "You're telling me." She nodded at one of her rats, who let out a long, piercing whistle. Within seconds the yellow-eyed rat emerged from a corridor, followed by former Kill Army High Majors Foiber and Schnauss, along with their cohorts from the prison corridor. Armed with knives and clubs, they rushed the city square.

Citizens screamed as Schnauss made his way down the aisle, snarling and spitting just as he had in the Catacombs, his dead eye drifting aimlessly in its socket. Dragging his loose, hairless skin, Foiber stomped behind him, cursing, waving his knife recklessly. Citizens cowered in their chairs, parents shielded their little ones.

"Thank you, High Major Ragwort," said Hecate as the yellow-eyed rat approached her.

He nodded with deference. "Yes, High Minister."

Schnauss and Foiber grinned cunningly at Juniper. "This somehow feels *familiar*," remarked Foiber. "I was in this exact situation years ago, only it was you who did the surprising back then. My, how the tables have turned. I'd spend a lifetime in your prison corridor to have this moment of satisfaction, to see the stupefied look upon your scarred face."

Hecate looked at Vincent, who shifted anxiously on his feet, eyeing Juniper for a signal. "Texi, if you please, hold your knife to Vincent's throat."

"What?" said Texi. "I—I can't. Elvi, please."

"You will be helping him," replied Hecate, "allowing him to remain unharmed. Young male rats are unpredictable. They sometimes do silly things which will get them . . . *hurt*."

Swallowing, Clover nodded at Texi. "It's all right, Texi," she said in the calmest voice she could muster. She let go of Vincent's paw. "Do as she says."

Of his own accord, Vincent took two steps down, allowing Texi to stand above him on the stairs and hold the knife to his throat. "I'm so sorry," she said weakly.

"Don't be sorry, Texi," whispered Vincent. "You're doing nothing wrong. It's Elvi—or whatever her name is—who is to blame. She's tricked all of us. Please, don't let her trick you again."

Ulrich couldn't take it anymore. He was distraught that he'd never spotted Elvi's deception, and that she'd had her hooks in Texi all this time. He bolted to his feet. "Do you really think your little scheme will work?" he shouted. "Do you really think we'll allow you to go back to the old ways?" Two guards grabbed for him, as did Ragan, trying to stop his brother from getting hurt. "High Minister, my backside!" A guard punched him in the ribs, but he would not relent. "Trilok was the real High Minister—the *only* High Minister!" The guard kicked

Ragan in the chest, hurling him back in his chair, while the other tripped Ulrich, knocking him to the ground, an ax aimed at his forehead.

"Ulrich!" yelled Texi.

Hecate held up her paw. "It's all right," she said to the guard. "Let *former* Chief of Security Ulrich speak." The guards dragged Ulrich to his feet and pushed him in front of her. Her mouth curved into a satisfied smirk as she spoke. "After all, if I'm not mistaken, it was you and your brother who enjoyed my tea *most* of all."

Her words struck Ulrich like a slap to the face. He stood before her and closed his eyes for a moment. Why had he never picked up on it before? He should have known! "The tea," he said dimly, trying to keep himself together. "All along, it was your tea. It clouded our thoughts, didn't it? Softened our judgment, bending us to your will."

"Ah, at long last one of you fools figures it out," said Hecate. "You're a real detective, aren't you? Too bad it took you so long." She smiled at Texi. "These rats don't deserve you. They have no spirit, not like yours, my little lion."

The majors laughed as Texi trembled, trying to blink her tears away. Ulrich looked up at her. "Texi, don't listen to her, understand?" He looked at the other Council members. "We're your friends. We care about you. She only cares about herself."

"You all but *gave* her to me," said Hecate. "None of you wanted to be troubled with poor pitiful Texi anymore. All of you were only too glad to shove her off on me!"

"Shut your deceitful mouth!" shouted Ulrich. "We trusted you. Texi admired you, but it was all a lie! Why, that senseless moth you keep caged in your quarters is of more value than you! You are nothing to her—you are nothing to any of us!"

In a flash, Hecate took the knife aimed at Juniper and

slashed Ulrich across his cheek, cutting him all the way to his lip.

"How's that for nothing?" she said.

He let out a wrathful howl, grabbing the side of his face, his paw quickly drenched in blood. He snarled at her and spat disdainfully on her feet.

Vincent yelled from the altar, "I spent most of my young life in the Catacombs, afraid every second, but no more! I for one will never be afraid again!" He looked right at Hecate. "I *knew* you were up to something all along! I always knew! Everyone, fight back—fight for our home!"

Major Ragwort bolted up the stairs to the altar. He growled angrily, diving fist-first onto Vincent, hitting him squarely in the jaw. "It's our home now, rat!" Clover rushed the major, plowing into his chest as Vincent hit the floor. Victor joined her; grabbing Ragwort by his ears, he wrenched the major down face-first to the floor.

Juniper wasted no time. He grabbed Hecate by the arm and reached for her knife, trying to twist it from her paw. Hecate screeched wildly, kicking and thrashing. With her free paw she clawed at Juniper's face, ripping at his eye patch.

In a flash Mother Gallo came at Hecate, sinking her teeth into her wrist before the dagger could make contact with Juniper's face. Hecate screamed for Foiber and Schnauss, who lunged at Mother Gallo with their weapons, but the Council had already jumped into the fray. They were unarmed; their claws would have to do.

Jumping onto his chair, Cole kicked a major in the snout and leaped on top of Schnauss, grabbing him around his waist and hurling the menacing high major to ground. He slashed at Schnauss's face with his claws, striking him in the nose until he heard bone crack. Schnauss moaned in pain, dropping his dagger as he tried to cover his face. Foiber came for Cole, his knife plunging into the floor over and over as Cole writhed on the ground trying to get Schnauss's dagger, the knife barely missing him each time. Foiber laughed as though it were a game. Virden came from behind him and grabbed folds of his sagging, hairless skin, twisting it tight. The major screamed, cursing and spitting as Virden twisted the skin behind his neck. Foiber threw his arms up, clawing at Virden's face. Cole snatched up Schnauss's dagger and ripped into Foiber's thigh with it, cutting him down to the bone.

Foiber fell to the ground, dragging himself into an aisle for protection. "You mangy Loyalists! You sickening, spineless hairballs!"

Cole laughed riotously. "You yellow-bellied, foul-mouthed sack of plague-ridden flesh, cowering on your knees among the rats you once so proudly abused!" Citizens came at Foiber from all sides, kicking him in the ribs, digging the claws of their feet into his cracked, infected skin as Hecate's rats jumped on top of the citizens, pulling them off the high major.

"Fight back, everyone!" shouted Carn, elbowing a major in the head as Oleander clawed at his back. "This is *our* home!"

The citizens needed no further encouragement. Packs of Hecate's soldiers came at them from all sides. Citizens kicked and clawed, dodging blades as best they could. Frightened parents fought back, protecting their little ones, their bodies and paws cut and beaten from blocking the many blows.

Mother Gallo searched for her children. The older boys were helping the Council fight off the armed rats, while Hob and Suttor's brother Kar were under their chairs, Tuk and Gage shielding them from harm. "Where are they?" she whispered, searching through the chaos. A lump formed in her throat at the sudden realization that they were nowhere to be seen. "Juniper, they're gone! The children—where are they?"

Juniper whipped around in a circle, his adrenaline and fear impelling him to shove Hecate's rats out of his way, his arms and body slashed and bleeding from their blades. He called his children's names, but neither answered. Suddenly there was a stabbing scream. Juniper's hackles rose, his whole body flooding with terror. He turned in time to see Foiber holding both Nomi and Julius in one arm, his claws digging into Julius's neck.

"Papa!" yelled Julius, his white coat smeared with blood from Foiber's bleeding leg. Nomi cried and squirmed as Foiber squeezed her small belly.

Her knife soaked in blood, Hecate bounded on top of a chair and gazed down smugly as Foiber shook the children. "Always using that bald head of yours, Major Foiber. Go for the runts—good thinking!"

"No!" blurted Juniper, holding up his paws in surrender. "Hecate, *please* . . . leave the children unharmed." Foiber snorted with pleasure, watching Juniper plead for his children's lives. "I beg of you, let them go. They are not part of this fight."

"That's what Killdeer thought of your Nightshade boys, and look where that got him. He's dead and buried, while those two mongrels have a city named after them," said Hecate.

Foiber snorted with delight as Julius kicked and screamed, trying to break free. "High Minister Hecate is right—better safe than sorry." He lifted his claws to Julius's throat. "One swipe on his tender little neck and the boy's done for—one less Loyalist for us to worry about!"

Foiber was poised to strike, when a paralyzing growl suddenly filled his ear. Icy cold breath, followed by long yellowed claws, slithered around his neck. Hecate's eyes widened with shock, her knife quivering in her paw. "Don't move an inch!" ordered the rat in a raspy voice. Foiber's whole body drained of color, his hairless skin now a deathly gray.

What looked to be arrows flew across the city square, planting themselves in the throats and hearts of unsuspecting rats, who fell to the ground squirming and sputtering and then simply stopped moving.

Gaping, Juniper looked on, unable to speak.

"Now then, Major Foiber," declared the rat evenly, "put my son down . . . my little niece, too."

The square seemed to take a collective breath. Citizens cried out in horror. Every soul stood still, staring breathlessly at the imposing rat in the center of the room.

With a crafty smirk, Billycan stared at Juniper. "If I remember correctly, you surprised me this way once upon a time."

"It's . . . it's all right!" Juniper called out to the citizens, his voice returning. "I promise you on my life. He means no harm."

"As I'm sure you remember," said Billycan, still clutching Foiber by the neck, "I *loathe* repeating myself, so Major, if I were you I'd do as I was told." With great care, Foiber set both children on the ground. Billycan gave him a belittling pat on his hairless head. "There's a good fellow."

Julius and Nomi bolted to their mother, hiding behind her legs.

As the citizens stifled their gasps, more rats moved into the square—foreign rats—surrounding them on all sides. A mass of rangy, ragtag rats, with silver rings piercing their ears, enclosed the square. Each one held a sizable crossbow, but strangely enough the arrows were not aimed at the citizens; they were trained on Hecate and her majors. The fallen rats with the arrows protruding from their lifeless forms were not Nightshade rats. They were the enemy.

"Guards, detain them," ordered Billycan. The armed rats swarmed around the majors, taking their weapons and forcing them to their knees, abruptly boxing ears and cuffing those who did not comply. They ripped Hecate off her chair, throwing her to the ground, her imperious smile gone.

"Brother," said Juniper, "how did you—"

"Did you honestly think I would miss a good fight?" asked Billycan.

"Not since I've known you," Juniper replied, exhaling.

Two armed rats stood on either side of Billycan. He gave them a nod. "Take him." He released his grasp on Foiber's fleshy neck. "Oh, I see he's injured," he said, frowning at the major's bleeding leg. "Do not tend to that wound. Let it get as infected as his rotting hide." The rats grabbed the suddenly speechless Foiber roughly, pushing him down the aisle.

After Hecate's rats had been restrained, Billycan gestured for her. She screeched and kicked and spat as she was forced in front of him. Indifferent to her protests, he folded his arms and regarded her. "You would have made Killdeer quite proud today." He tilted his head, a hint of satisfaction spreading across his mouth. "Well, *almost* proud. You failed, after all."

"I should have finished you off last year!" said Hecate. "You and your bloody nine lives—like a flea-bitten alley cat!"

"Hecate, since I've known you, your biggest fault has always been your arrogance. Last year, during our little *tussle* in my cell, you should have made quite sure I was dead. Had you done so, you'd be looking at Killdeer's throne right now. When I took my leave of Trillium, I was sure Juniper would be on to you soon. It wasn't until I found out about your little prank—your *delightful* tea—that I truly became concerned. Thankfully, my

Toscan friends have no love for their former empress and were more than happy to tell me all about your little experiments on their isolated island."

Hecate's spite shifted to disbelief. "You—you were in *Tosca*?"

Tilting his head, he clasped his paws together theatrically. "Ajax and Silvius send their warmest regards. Oh, how they miss you."

"Ajax is useless and Silvius is a mad old fool! I should know—I made him that way!"

"To be sure, you've done damage to Silvius, but he's by no means mad. If you'd taken care of him and Ajax properly, I'd still be in Tosca, none the wiser. Again, Hecate, your arrogance, your fatal flaw, has tripped you up."

A wounded voice cut the air. "No!" it shouted from a nearby corridor. "Duncan, no!"

Cole, Vincent, and Juniper bolted through the crowd, stumbling over fallen rats, pushing their way to the entrance of the corridor.

Suttor was on his knees at the entrance to the corridor, his head resting on Duncan's still chest. He was crying, pounding the ground with his fists. Overcome, Cole dropped down next to him.

"Bless the Saints!" said Juniper. "What happened here?"

"I don't know!" exclaimed Suttor. "Everything was fine. Duncan was with me, having tea, in the prison corridor. All of a sudden I didn't feel so good—dizzy, sick to my stomach—and then everything went black. When I came to, all the cells were empty and I found him lying here." He looked at Cole. "Father, help me! We must do something. He won't wake up!"

"Suttor must have been slipped something," said Cole, putting his arm around him, "in Hecate's tea." He clutched Duncan's motionless paw. "That's how they all escaped."

"Did Duncan have tea, too?" asked Vincent.

Suttor searched his mind, working through the foggy jumble of what occurred. "I can't remember. It's all a blur."

"Let's get him to Virden," said Juniper. He ripped off his cloak and laid it on the ground. "Gently now, we must lift him."

The four rats placed Duncan on Juniper's cloak, now a makeshift stretcher. "Virden!" called Juniper. "We need you. It's Duncan!" They moved through the crowd and when they reached the center aisle, they laid Duncan at the base of the altar.

Suttor knelt at his brother's side and spoke to him as Virden listened to his chest and checked for any signs of life. "Please, Duncan, you must wake up," he whispered. "You've so much to do. You're going to take us through the museum, remember?" He wiped away tears. "You're going to be somebody . . . somebody important, like I always knew you would."

Glancing up at Juniper, Virden shook his head. He could feel no pulse. Clover took Kar in her arms. He buried his face in her shoulder while Cole held Lali back from Duncan's body, her grief-stricken cries muffled against his chest.

A rat began to laugh.

Suttor jumped to his feet, his pain turning to rage. "What are you laughing at, rat?"

Major Ragwort's yellow eyes glinted. He leered from the top of the altar down at Duncan. "With the lack of brains on that heap of orange fluff, I did the world a service—gave him a right thrashing, I did!" He laughed. "You're lucky you're not lying there next to him, boy!"

Suttor flew forward, leaping over his brother and onto Ragwort, knocking him and the rats detaining him to the ground. He grabbed Ragwort's throat. Juniper, Carn, and Victor jumped on top of him, desperately trying to peel him off, but he would not relent. With a swift kick in the chin from Suttor, Carn tumbled back, knocking into one of the rats holding Hecate. She took her chance. With one arm free she dived for the ground, sweeping up the fallen rat's crossbow and striking the other guard detaining her with the heavy end. Now free, she twisted around and took aim, launching the heavy arrow into the scuffling rats just before two citizens tackled her.

"Uncle!" screamed Clover, clutching Kar to her chest.

Stumbling, Juniper lurched forward, bumping into Vincent, and clutched his stomach.

"Juniper?" Vincent seized Juniper trying to steady him as he wobbled. "He's hit!" he shouted. "Juniper's hit!"

Victor grabbed for Suttor, still struggling to get hold of Ragwort. "Suttor, stop!" he shouted. "It's Juniper!"

Suttor wouldn't listen. Victor jumped from the altar, landing on Suttor's back, managing to get him in a choke hold. Growling, he held down Suttor's arms until he finally stopped flailing. "Juniper's been hit. Snap out of it!" he barked. "You *must* get hold of yourself! Look around you! Your brother's not the only one who lost his life tonight, and Juniper may be next!"

At last Suttor stopped struggling. From his vantage point on the floor, he could see all the devastation that had occurred— devastation he had not noticed before. Puddles of blood were soaking into the floor; blood smeared the hanging flowers. Several rats were lying on the ground in crumpled positions. They were not moving.

Reaching down, Juniper felt the arrow protruding from his stomach. Grabbing hold of the blood-slickened wood, he yanked it from his belly, grunting as he did so.

"Papa!" cried Julius as Mother Gallo held him back.

"Steady, now," said Virden. He and Vincent guided Juniper to the nearest chair. "Let me have a look."

"No," blurted Juniper. "I—I think I'm all right."

"Not with that much blood, you're not."

"Please, Juniper," said Vincent, "don't be foolish."

"It—it looks bad, I know," said Juniper, panting. "Knocked the wind out of me, to be sure. But . . ." He opened his satchel. He pulled out a round silver tag—the one he always kept with him as a reminder, his brother's lab tag. It had been damaged, the edge of it nicked by an arrow. With some difficulty he pulled the strap over his head and turned the satchel over. It had a hole though and through. He smiled dimly at Julius and Nomi, who clutched their mother, looking on in sheer terror. With a groan, Juniper sat up a bit so they could see the wound. "See, it looks far worse than it is." He glanced at Billycan, holding up the tag for his children. "This tag—it saved my life."

After wiping away the blood, Virden inspected the size and location of the wound. He nodded at Mother Gallo. "The old chap's right," he said.

Mother Gallo let out a long breath. "Thank you," she whispered.

Hecate suddenly made a strange sound, a bubbling,

gurgling sort of sound. She grabbed at her throat. Choking, she removed her paws, revealing a silver dagger buried up to the hilt. The guards holding her let go, and she fell to the ground, thrashing briefly, and then she simply stopped.

Juniper regarded her on the ground. She was dead. He looked at Billycan. "We had her under control. Which one of your rats did this?"

Billycan looked down at her body with little concern. "Honestly, brother, she just tried to kill you." He shook his head. "Besides, these rats don't use knives. They didn't do this."

"Then who did?"

Ripping off her dirtied yellow sash and letting it fall to the ground, Texi stepped down from the altar. "It was me."

"Texi, why?" asked Juniper. "The rats had her detained."

"When you got hit, I watched her from the altar. She looked right at me, smiling like a fox. I saw a flash of something in her paw. I . . . I thought it was a weapon." She sniffled. "She always told me—one of her 'life lessons'—that sometimes our enemies are staring us right in the face and we just don't know it." She wiped her eyes. "This time I knew. It was her."

Vincent looked at Hecate's body, nudging a limp arm with his foot. He reached down and picked up a small silver blade, small enough to conceal with little difficulty. He held it up. "She was going to finish the job, Juniper."

"She may not always make the kill, but she never misses," said Billycan, "I'll give her that."

"You saved my life," said Juniper, looking down at Texi. "You could have helped Hecate, but you didn't." He knelt down and raised her quivering chin. "You're a good rat who does the right thing." A slight smile formed on her mouth. "And knowing that is the greatest life lesson of all."

"Duncan!" shouted Suttor, crawling over to his brother.

Duncan was sitting up, leaning on his elbows, looking around the square.

"Are you all right?" asked Suttor.

"I think so. My head hurts . . . and I'm hungry."

"He's definitely all right," said Victor.

Pushing through the crowd, Lali fell to her knees and grabbed him by the shoulders. "Don't ever do that to me again!" she exclaimed. "Do you understand me?" Duncan nodded, squirming slightly, as Lali kissed him all over his face. "Never again."

"What happened in the prison corridor?" asked Suttor.

Feeling the lump on his head, Duncan swallowed hard. "Elvi suggested I bring tea to Suttor, to get over my fear of the prison corridor." He looked up at Juniper. "When I unlocked the door, I thought the rat was another guard. I . . . I didn't know." He eyed the bodies of rats lying on the ground. "I caused all this."

"Duncan, this wasn't your fault," said Juniper.

Silently, Cole gathered Kar from Clover and walked over to his family. He got down on one knee. "You caused nothing, son. She did. This was all her doing, not yours. She used you."

Juniper looked around the city square, taking in the dubious horde of rats Billycan had brought with him. "Billycan, where did all these rats *come* from? Where did you find them?"

Before he could answer, Billycan felt a gentle tugging on his leg. He bent down and scooped up Julius in his arms. "How are you, lad?" he asked. "My, how you've grown."

"Father, where have you been?"

"I've been to a great island, a mysterious island, in a dangerous land."

"Did you see tigers?" asked Julius curiously.

Billycan chuckled. "I saw something far more important than mere tigers—especially to *us*."

"What was it?"

"I met a rat who looks *just* like you and me."

"You mean . . . another albino?" Julius asked in a whisper. Billycan nodded. The little rat shivered. "*Just* like us?"

"Precisely like us. I'll tell you all about him later." He glanced at Juniper. "Julius, there is someone I need you to meet."

The sea of armed rats broke, clearing the center aisle, revealing a lean brown rat. Unlike the others, she was majestic—polished. Her gait was refined, and even the tilt of her sleek head seemed noble.

As she stopped before him, Julius gazed up at her. He held out a small white paw, feeling as though he must use his best manners, as his mother had taught him, with a lady such as this. "I'm Julius," he said. "A pleasure to meet you."

She glanced at Billycan, a troubled look on her face. "I know who you are," she said, leaning down toward Julius. "I've heard all about you."

"You have?"

"Yes, I'm told by Billycan you're a very brave young rat— that you faced down Killdeer's sisters all on your own."

Looking down at his feet, Julius blushed. "Well . . . Texi was with me." He looked back at her big eyes. "What's your name?

"My name is Gwenfor."

"Where do you live?"

"Topside." She gestured at the armed rats. "We live on the docks at the Hellgate Sea."

"But I thought the dock rats were cutthroats—pirates of the sea," he said. "You look too beautiful. Are you *really* a dock rat?"

She nodded. "Just like my mother and father before me, now I lead the dock rats." Her face looked uneasy again. "It seems you, too, were born from leaders."

Mother Gallo suddenly clutched Juniper's arm. She hadn't seen it at first. She hadn't been looking. It wasn't until Gwenfor was face to face with Julius that she noticed her jaw was the same angular shape as his. His long snout resembled Billycan's, but it had the same distinctive slope as Gwenfor's. His eyes were perfect almonds—just like hers.

"Filthy dock rats!" shouted Major Ragwort from the altar where he was being detained. He spat blood, his mouth still bleeding from Suttor's attack. "You reek of salt and sewer water!" One of the dock rats holding him smacked the back of his head, but it didn't stop his raving. "Killdeer should have gone through with his plan to eradicate you all those years ago."

Ignoring Ragwort, Gwenfor turned to Juniper. "Chief Citizen, let me take these shameful excuses for rats away from this place." Foiber cursed her from the aisle, his captors tightening their hold. "Trust me, they will get *exactly* what they deserve." She looked down at Julius. "And they will never bother your family again."

"Gwenfor, we are most grateful for your help," said Juniper. "If there is ever anything I can do to repay the favor, you need only ask." He glanced at the captured rats. "As for this ragged lot, we have plenty of room in our prison corridor. Trust me, they won't get out a second time."

"Very well," said Gwenfor. "I suppose our work is done." She bent down and leaned in very close to Julius. Her voice was stern. "Now listen to me. The world above your head is no place for you, little rat. It's perilous and full of threats, but it is also my home. So if ever you find yourself Topside with no safe place to go, simply sniff the air and let the smell of salt bring you to me." Gingerly she took his chin in her paw. "You stay with your papa and mama, do you hear me? They will look out for you." Hesitantly, she kissed the top of his head, then stood up. "Chief Citizen, my rats and I will escort these criminals to your prison corridor."

Juniper nodded to Ulrich and Ragan, who began leading the prisoners out of the city square. "Thank you," he said. He glanced at Julius. "For everything."

"Where I live, a son of mine would be a target for any rat wanting to claim my command."

"You are free to see him anytime you like."

"No," said Gwenfor decisively. "It's better this way." She watched the children crowding around Mother Gallo. "You are very lucky. You lead your city and are still able to keep your family close."

Juniper could see Gwenfor's chin trembling. The dock rats were a proud clan. He changed the subject. "Perhaps we can help each other. Gwenfor, have any of your rats gone missing?"

Gwenfor's hackles rose. "What do you mean, *missing*?"

"Nightshade has had three teams of our Hunter rats disappear in the last few weeks. My Hunters are smart. They would never allow themselves to be taken unless it was beyond their control."

"I'm missing nearly twenty," said Gwenfor gravely. "My rats never leave the docks without my permission. I will not allow it. That's how I keep them alive." She exhaled. "I must admit, I had become lenient. I had rats doing their rounds well into the early hours—easy to spot. A dozen went missing. I sent my best trackers into Trillium to find them. Now they're gone, too."

Juniper was almost relived to hear the news. At the very least, he knew it wasn't just Nightshade rats who were being targeted. It was a cruel comfort. He took in the room. Nearly every citizen was staring at Billycan, many trembling—still haunted by memories of the Catacombs, more afraid of him, the one who had just saved their lives, than they could ever be of Hecate. How could he prove to them that they were safe, that Billycan was no longer out to destroy them?

CHAPTER EIGHT
The City Morque

ARMS FOLDED, Vincent leaned against a wall and silently took in the hushed scene. He glanced around the Council Chamber for Victor, who was strangely absent.

Carn and Ragan whispered in a corner, shaking their heads, feeling foolish that they never suspected Elvi, their thoughts clouded by her toxic tea.

Mother Gallo, Oleander, and Clover sat in a tight circle, talking quietly about the damage done—and how, even from beyond the grave, Killdeer's tyrannical reign had claimed lives, both of his loyal followers and of innocent Nightshade rats.

Virden broke the stillness.

"For Saints' sake, stop moving," he barked, "or this needle will end up in your forehead!" Ulrich squirmed as Virden tended to the large gash running across his face. "Why, Juniper took it in the stomach and didn't say a word when I stitched him up."

Ulrich grunted in response.

"Don't be so hard on him," said Texi, holding one of Ulrich's paws in her own. "What he did was very, very brave." Ulrich moaned in pain, trying to smile at her.

"Indeed it *was* brave," said Virden. He chuckled. "If only our stubby-tailed friend could have that same bravery now." He tied off the final stitch. "There, good as new."

With great difficulty Ulrich stretched out his jaw, gently feeling the black stitching with the underside of his paw.

Texi held up a small mirror for him. "It's not bad," she said, mustering her most hopeful smile. "Quite distinguished, really."

"Bless the Saints!" Ulrich exclaimed. "I'm absolutely appalling!" He sighed miserably and glanced around the room. "A fine rat I am, grousing over a cut on my face. What of those who lost their lives tonight?"

Virden patted his shoulder. "Don't be so hard on yourself, old fellow. The High Ministry is defeated at last."

"Ha!" shouted Vincent, springing up from his leaning position as Juniper and Billycan entered the Council Chamber. "We thought that once before!" His chest began to heave. "The cloud of the High Ministry will always hang over our heads. Even now, *he's* back." He growled in Billycan's direction. "He *may* have changed, but how can we be sure? He, even more than Killdeer, was responsible for all the murders over the years— the murders of our families, our friends! We cannot dare trust him! We trusted Elvi, and look where that got us. Now we're supposed to believe he's a changed rat? It *never* ends! Never!"

Vincent closed his eyes, waiting for the earnest, hopeful words that only Juniper could summon. He'd heard them all before. Juniper's heart was always in the right place, but his goodness, his need to do right by all, was often infuriating. Vincent had always reasoned, now more than ever, that sometimes you *had* to be unkind; sometimes you must rule with an iron fist, not to be cruel but to ensure the lives of your people.

"Where is Victor?" he asked sharply. "Wasn't he with you? He should be here."

"I don't know, son," said Juniper calmly.

"Has *anyone* seen my brother?" demanded Vincent, glaring around the chamber.

"I have," said Billycan.

"You?"

"I know where he is. I'll take you to him."

"You can walk next to me," said Billycan, eyeing Vincent from the corner of his eye. "I won't bite."

Vincent wasn't taking any chances. He followed Billycan cautiously down a winding corridor to the lowest level of Nightshade City, all the while keeping a firm hold on the blade he'd taken from one of Hecate's fallen henchmen. "I'm quite fine where I am, thank you."

"Suit yourself," replied Billycan without a hint of emotion.

"Where are you taking me?" Before Billycan could answer, the scent hit Vincent's snout. It was scent he knew all too well— the scent of death.

"Here we are," said Billycan as they rounded a corner. They came upon a long, thin room. Except for one flickering torch, it was dark and deathly still—the city morgue.

In all the time he'd been in Nightshade, Vincent had never been to this part of the city, perhaps purposely staying away from the one place that he knew would force all the horrible memories of the Catacombs to come flooding back. Why would Victor be here?

Hesitantly, Vincent followed Billycan into the dim chamber. He'd learned to be afraid of little, but death always unnerved him, the finality of it all. He believed in the Saints, but sometimes he wondered if they were real.

His eyes adjusting to the dark, he spotted Victor's dark frame sitting on the ground, leaning back against the wall. He seemed to be looking at nothing. "Victor," he whispered, crouching down. "Why are you here, by yourself? This is no place for you. It's no place for anyone."

Listlessly, Victor turned his attention to his brother. "I should have done more."

Vincent forced himself to look at the many shrouded bodies, all alive and happy just hours ago, attending *his* wedding. There were thirty, maybe more. "Victor, there was nothing you or anyone could do. We were ambushed." Glancing over at Billycan, who waited near the door, he lowered his voice. "It seems there will always be tragedy wherever we go. From now on, we must trust no one. We must concentrate on staying alive, just like we did in the Catacombs."

"You make it all sound so grim," said Victor.

Vincent exhaled and glanced around the chamber. "It is."

"I need to do something," said Victor. "I need to make a difference."

"There's nothing any of us can do right now but mourn our dead and carry on as best we can." Vincent shook his head glumly. "As we always have."

"No!" said Victor, springing to his feet. "No!" He pushed Vincent in the chest. "You, of all rats, to sound so defeated. What's happened to you? When did you become such a broken rat, always expecting the worst?"

Vincent growled. "Mind your words, brother."

"I'm sick to death of minding my words. I'm sick to death of it!" He shoved past Vincent.

"Where are you going?" Vincent demanded.

"To do something!"

"To do what?"

"Something important!"

"Victor, stop!"

"Out of my way," commanded Victor, glaring at Billycan.

"Wait," said Billycan, blocking Victor's path. "Leaving in this state can lead to nothing but trouble."

"You, of all rats, have no right to stop me from doing *anything*!" said Victor, growling contemptuously. "Now move!"

Suddenly Billycan snarled. His yellow teeth bared, he shouted, "I have more right than anyone!" Vincent came forward, his sword ready to strike. "I know the terror my temper brought upon many a rat!" said Billycan. "I live with it every day! I dream of it every night!" He pushed Victor back farther into the darkened chamber, his eyes aglow with red fury. "I must live with the horrors of my past. The blood that lies squarely on my claws—your family's blood, the blood of your father, my son's namesake! Never tell me I have *no right*! I know personally how destructive rage and wrath can be!" Billycan's chest heaved, white froth bubbling from his mouth.

Victor reached for his brother, clutching his shoulder as hard as he could. Panting, he asked, "If you really care . . . tell me what you'd do to bring back our father? What would you do to bring back Julius Nightshade?"

Taking a long breath, Billycan stepped back. "Your father . . . had he not been killed—by me—there would have never been a High Ministry. He wouldn't have allowed it, that I am sure of. If I could bring him back, I would condemn myself to the most ghastly torture you could dream of—a torture so profound I would beg for death, but never receive it."

"Why . . . why did you despise him so much?" asked Victor.

"I suppose because he was everything I was not. He was

generous, principled, honorable. He was good." Billycan's smile vanished. "He was beloved."

Vincent stood speechless at the thought that Billycan might actually be telling . . . the *truth*. If the former High Collector had wanted any Nightshade rat dead, they'd have died last year back in the Catacombs, when Killdeer's crazed sisters tried to reclaim control. Billycan wouldn't have journeyed to Tosca, and he surely wouldn't have stopped Hecate and the former high majors from regaining control. Naturally it could be some twisted ruse; Billycan was as smart as he was deadly. But to what end? He had had two recent opportunities to see *all* of Nightshade's leaders dead—Loyalist filth, as he used to call them—but here they all were, alive and well.

Vincent turned to his brother, who still clutched his shoulder. He could feel Victor's paw shaking, his claws digging into his skin. He didn't know if it was from anger, fear, or a combination of the two, but his brother's whole body trembled. "It's all right, Victor," he said softly. "You've nothing to be afraid of."

"I'm not afraid," said Victor.

"Then . . . what is it?"

"You've always told me that Father said our lives need to mean something," said Victor. "And the only way to change our fate is to change our lives."

"Yes," replied Vincent. "Father never gave up, not even in the darkest of hours. He was a firm believer in fate."

"Well then, there's no more to be said." With that, Victor pushed past Billycan and bolted from the room.

Billycan woke with a start, drenched in sweat. He grabbed his head. "No," he muttered, "please. Make it stop!"

He had been dreaming, an endless nightmare of blood and death he couldn't pull himself out of. Visions of needles and cages filled with dead rats. Rats screaming in agony. Rats screaming his name, begging for mercy.

He pulled himself off the long cot he'd been given to sleep on, hidden away in a vacant quarters where the still fearful citizens wouldn't come across him. He dragged himself to a shard of mirror, leaning against the wall, all the while pulling at his ears, hoping it might send the horrible thoughts out of his head. Slowly he raised his head and looked at himself. He dropped to his knees. His eyes were a brilliant, torrid orange—a hue he'd not seen in a very long time.

Turning away from the mirror, he noticed his door was ajar. Cautiously he stepped into the dim corridor. Deep claw marks traveled from his door all the way down the corridor. The word "KILL" was scrawled above them in crooked capital letters. He followed the claw marks to a set of stairs that led up to Nightshade Passage. Bits of paper covered the stairwell, as though someone had furiously shredded it.

Billycan picked up a scrap of paper and studied it. It was a page from one of the scientists' diaries. He picked up another piece, trying to read the words. All he could make out were the words "rats," "intellect," and "human-like."

He froze. He smelled a rat at the top of the stairs. He could hear its shaky breaths. "Who's there?" he called out.

No one answered. He heard only footsteps running away.

He looked down at his claws. They were covered in earth, and several were bleeding. He stretched out his digits and fitted them into the claw marks on the dirt wall—a perfect match.

* * *

Vincent, Virden, and Juniper sat in the Council Chamber, listening to Billycan's news of Silvius's findings.

"Silvius believes the volcano holds the secret of who we are," continued Billycan. "And that's what the Topsiders have been after all this time."

Virden did the math in his head, and then yanked the quill pen from behind his ear, furiously scribbling numbers in his notebook. He dropped the pen onto the notebook. "Why, humans could live over a thousand years!"

"Bless the Saints," said Juniper. "Do you know how precious a commodity that would be? They'd pay anything—risk anything—to get it."

Billycan nodded. "All those years I spent in the lab, there was more going on than just the testing of the drug I was given. Silvius was never given any injections. Instead, he and many more were all but butchered—the Topsiders took their blood, their flesh, to find out what makes Trillium rats tick."

"In the diaries we found from the scientists, they state how our traits are in many ways more like humans than rats," said Juniper.

The door to the Council Chamber suddenly rattled.

"Who's there?" asked Juniper, rising from his chair.

"It's Petra," said a meek voice from the other side of the door.

"Petra?" said Vincent. He scratched his head, wondering why Victor's sweetheart would be knocking on the door.

Juniper, just as curious, opened the door, and the little blond rat stepped inside, her face creased with worry. "My dear, what are you doing here? Is Victor all right?"

Petra talked so rapidly no one could make out any more than the words "Victor" and "good-bye."

"You must slow down," said Vincent soothingly. He got up from his chair and crouched in front of her. "Catch your breath, then talk. Tell us what happened to Victor."

Trembling, Petra gulped in a breath of air and blew it out, doing this two more times before she could talk. "I'm—I'm not sure what happened," she finally got out. "He came to our quarters to say *good-bye*! He said he had to do something brave—to change fate—like his father did. He said he would find the missing Hunters, pledged to bring them back alive!"

"The missing . . ." repeated Juniper. "The missing Hunters—he's gone to find them. He's gone Topside!"

"Petra, was anyone with him?" asked Vincent. "Do you know where he was headed Topside?"

She shook her head. "He was alone. He left so quickly. I'm sorry."

"Did he say anything else?" asked Juniper. "Anything at all?"

"Well . . . yes," said Petra, "but I didn't really understand it." Her brow knitted as she tried to remember the exact wording. "He said something about Duncan, what he'd told him, about a museum. I'm not sure I can remember exactly. It all happened so fast."

"Try!" barked Billycan, bolting up in his chair, jolted by the mention of the museum.

Jumping, Petra gave a small yelp, and grabbed Vincent's arm.

Billycan lowered his voice. "Please, *try* to remember what he said. It's most important."

"It's all right," whispered Vincent, patting her paw. "He might be able to help." He glanced at Juniper. "Juniper says Billycan has a talent for this sort of thing—tracking down rats. He can help us find Victor."

"Of course," said Petra stiffly. "He . . . he kept bringing up The Lords of Trillium. Duncan said it was some display in the museum—about the great leaders of Trillium and how they worked to build the city."

Billycan's flesh rose in goose bumps as his mind flashed back to the lab—to his only friend, Dorf. The little spotted rat had tried to explain to him that Trillium's great leaders were not great at all; they were criminals, stealing the land from the weak, leaving them to suffer and die. "Why would Victor be so interested in this particular display?"

"He said Duncan had lived in the museum once," said Petra, "that he'd heard other rats there, smelled them, too, in the museum, and their scents led him to The Lords of Trillium. Duncan said he was drawn to that spot in the museum, even before he sensed the other rats."

"But what would make him think the Hunters could be there?"

"He said he read something in one of the diaries," said Petra. "The ones the bats just brought us."

"He must have discovered the same thing Silvius did," said Vincent, "that the museum and the lab were connected. He always suspected the humans were to blame for the Hunters' disappearance. What better place to start looking for them?"

"Juniper, how do your Hunters journey to the surface?" asked Billycan.

"The south tunnel. They always start there, and fan out in teams once they reach Topside." Juniper eyed his brother. Both of them were thinking the same thing. "Petra, did you see which way Victor went?"

"Yes, I tried to go after him, but he was too fast. He took a left down our corridor. He never goes that way."

"Petra's corridor heads directly to the south tunnel," said Vincent.

"Where does it lead?" asked Billycan.

"Right to the heart of Trillium City."

"Well then, that's where we start," said Juniper. He looked at Vincent. "Gather the Council—Duncan, too."

CHAPTER NINE
Trillium

FOG, SLITHERING CLAWS OF CINDER, weaved its way through the streets and alleys of Trillium City, encasing everything in a tombstone gray.

Vincent and the other young rats, along with the original Council members except for Virden and the twins, who stayed back to attend to the wounded, trekked the long distance up the south tunnel into Trillium. They were armed with weapons recovered from Hecate's majors.

Despite anyone's doubts about his motives, Juniper knew the fastest way to track Victor was to follow the best huntsman he knew, a rat who could sniff out a wayward Kill Army recruit well before all others. He watched his brother intently as he sniffed the air.

"The heart," whispered Billycan, staring up at the Brimstone Building. Once he had stood in this very alley with his mother, Lenore, after she'd rescued him from the lab. She'd said the Topsiders called the Brimstone Building the heart of

Trillium City. He remembered how angry it had made him at the time—how he hated the Topsiders for controlling the rats and how he hated his own kind for allowing it to happen. He didn't feel angry now. He felt only a deep and hollow sadness. He sniffed the air, somehow thinking he might just catch a trace of his mother. Instead, he smelled something else entirely. He walked toward the Dumpster. "Blood . . . and Victor. He was here."

"Blood!" said Vincent nervously.

"It's not his," said Billycan. "It's not even rat—this blood is raccoon. I'm sure of it." Raccoons were despicable creatures, but their flesh was tender. He salivated as he touched the side of the Dumpster, rubbing the powdery dried blood between his digits.

"Even if it's not Victor's blood, he could still be hurt," said Vincent, thinking of the strong, lethal claws of a famished raccoon.

"This blood is old. Your brother and this fellow weren't here at the same time," said Billycan.

"I'm afraid we're responsible for that," said Juniper, looking at Vincent. "We came here searching for the Hunters, but met with an agitated raccoon instead."

Vincent sighed with relief, only now remembering the incident, which seemed so long ago. "Yes, with his rotten apples."

Billycan was impressed. A raccoon, in particular an irritated one, could be quite a challenge. "And what became of him?"

"You'll be disappointed to know that he escaped with his life," said Juniper. "If that's what you're asking."

"Just checking," Billycan replied with the barest hint of a smile. He sniffed the air and pointed down the alley. "Victor's scent leads this way."

Wrinkling his nose, Vincent sniffed the air. He could smell his brother, but the scent seemed to lead nowhere, evaporating within seconds.

"It's different with those closest to us," said Juniper, sensing his frustration. "Our fears tend to cloud our ability to track a scent clearly. When Julius went missing last year, I seemed to smell him everywhere and nowhere."

"Well, it's maddening," said Vincent, kicking an aluminum can. "Why would Victor do something so brash? Even for him, this was a foolish move."

"Your father was much like Victor, you know," said Juniper. "In his youth, he wasn't always one to think things through."

"The legendary Julius Nightshade was like Victor?" asked Suttor, astonished.

"Yes," added Cole, smirking, "there was many a time when Barcus had to hold Julius back from doing something reckless, from reacting before thinking."

"Indeed, my older brother had his hands full being best friends with Julius," Juniper added. "He outgrew it, of course, but knowing Julius in his younger days, Victor's behavior doesn't surprise me . . . not at all."

As the moon rose and the shadows climbed up the skyscrapers, the rats made their way unseen to the busiest street in the Battery District, the oldest and dirtiest part of Trillium. Watching as the massive cars and trucks blew past them, horns blaring, splashing dirty water, blinding them with flashing lights, Carn wondered if they were simply wandering. He was frustrated—not happy to be led by Billycan, of all rats, but more importantly, annoyed that no one *but* Billycan knew how to navigate the city. It made him feel helpless and beholden to the rat he'd grown up serving in the Catacombs. "We'll never find it," he said, batting a lump of broken asphalt with his sword. "Where do we even start?"

Running a paw over his face, Billycan let out a defeated sigh. "I thought we could make it there on foot, but it's taking far too much time."

"Well, I don't suppose you have an *alternative*?" asked Carn peevishly.

"Indeed I do," said Billycan, "though it may not be your preferred mode of transportation."

"Transportation," repeated Cole, not liking where this was going.

Billycan scratched his chin, pondering. "If anyone would still be alive," he muttered to himself, "it would have to be . . . the old geezer. He's got to be a fossil by now. . . ."

"What are you going on about?" asked Oleander, who was not at all at home in the city, wishing desperately they were searching for Victor back in the swamp, a place she knew.

Billycan's eyes glinted, taking in all the confused faces. "Words of advice: follow instructions to the letter, mind your tails, and above all, hold on to your stomachs."

Vincent's nose twitched, the smell of gasoline, exhaust, and grease invading his sinuses. It was a noisy city garage, with humans dashing about, working on cars, gassing up their grubby yellow cabs, cursing and shouting at each other.

"Stay to the wall," whispered Billycan as they made their way single file behind a rusted wall of shelving, stacked to the ceiling with tires, all crusted with dirt and salt. Billycan stopped as they reached another part of the garage, where taxicabs were pouring out into the street or careening back into the garage at breakneck speed.

Oleander shuddered. "No wonder you stay underground,"

she whispered to Clover. "You'd be lucky to live past childhood in such a hazardous place."

"You deal with deadly snakes on a daily basis," Clover pointed out.

"I'll take snakes over this any day."

"Listen, everyone, you must run on my signal—very, very fast," hissed Billycan. "You risk dying if you don't." Everyone's ears perked, their bodies ready for flight. Billycan snapped his head around. "Now!"

Just as a taxi pulled out into the street, he shot across the busy garage, the others racing behind.

Juniper, at the rear end of the line, watched in awe as a taxi came flying into the garage, missing Billycan's tail by just inches. How did he time it so perfectly? How often had he come to this place? It made Juniper wonder how much more there was to his brother than he'd ever know.

They raced after Billycan, who dived through an opening in a painted orange guardrail and dashed down a ramp. Panting, he came to a fast stop, the others nearly piling on top of one another as they came to a halt.

Vincent and Juniper rushed to Billycan's side. Vincent looked at the panting white rat, watching his face as it broke into . . . a smile. Not a sly smile or a cruel smile, but a *real* smile. Billycan didn't acknowledge him or Juniper. He merely looked down the ramp with what could only be happiness. Vincent followed his gaze, down the ramp to a yellow-lined curb of the garage. He was staring at a grizzled old rat. Suddenly the rat turned. His eyes met Billycan's. The rat's face went slack and

his ragged ears drooped. He was timeworn and bony, but agile. His head snapped this way and that, quickly taking in all the rats gathering behind Billycan. His shocked face cracked into a wide smile of broken teeth. He waved hurriedly from across the garage, leaping up and down as he beckoned Billycan over.

"How do you know that rat?" asked Juniper.

"I knew him in my younger days . . . before the Catacombs," whispered Billycan.

"Who is he?"

"That's Fitspur."

CHAPTER TEN

Fitspur

THE RAT FITSPUR BEGAN TO SHAKE when Billycan neared. At first glance one might have thought he was frightened, but a closer look showed he wasn't afraid in the least. He was over the moon. "Billycan, it really *is* you!" he shouted.

As Billycan hopped onto the curb, Fitspur snapped up his paw and shook it briskly. He spoke as fast as he moved. "And look at you — all grown up! You're a sight for sore eyes, to be sure." He shook his head, rebuking himself. "What am I doing, shaking your paw? This calls for a hug of epic proportions!" As old and skeletal as he was, Fitspur grabbed Billycan and squeezed him tightly. Billycan laughed out loud. The younger rats exchanged glances, looking at the odd scene in silence. This couldn't be happening—a rat, other than little Julius, actually happy to see . . . *Billycan*?

Juniper cleared his throat, getting Billycan's attention.

"Fitspur," said Billycan, "it's so good to see you, truly, but we're in a rush." He set a paw on Fitspur's shoulder. "I'll come back to see you soon, but a young rat is missing. We think he's gone to the City Museum, and I was hoping to enlist your services. Getting there on foot, without proper directions—well, we may be too late by the time we find him."

"My dear boy," said Fitspur, "no need to explain, none at all!"

"*Dear boy*," muttered Suttor. "He's got to be joking."

"Fitspur, this is my brother, Juniper."

Fitspur's crooked eyes looked as if they were about to pop from their sockets. "You mean—your *real* brother, your flesh and blood? You found family?" He grabbed Juniper's paw and shook it firmly. "It is a pleasure to meet you, indeed!" His eyes darted between Juniper and Billycan. "Why, you're exactly the same size, aren't you? How did you two meet? You must tell me everything!"

"Well, that's a long story," said Juniper.

"Very long, to be sure," said Billycan. "Fitspur, we really do need—"

"Yes, yes, of course!" said Fitspur. He glanced at the Nightshade rats surrounding Juniper and Billycan. "Ah . . . you're groundlings, then, aren't you?"

"*Groundlings?*" asked Juniper.

"Yes, groundlings. You live underground—in those tunnels. Why, I can spot a groundling a mile away. You all have that nervous, jittery look about you. Dead giveaway." He shuddered. "Too confining, if you ask me. I'd go a little wonky not being able to hear the noise of the city or breathe the fresh air."

Suttor elbowed Carn. "Has he smelled this place?"

Juniper smiled. He'd never thought of himself as a *groundling*. Other than the dock rats, there were few rats who lived above ground and made it to Fitspur's age. Clearly this rat was a tough old bird.

Fitspur let out a long, shrill whistle. Within seconds a slender gray rat dashed around a corner. All Fitspur said to her was "City Museum." She nodded her head and darted back the other way. "C'mon, then," he said, giving the Nightshade rats a crafty grin. His eyes glinted. "Let's get this show on the *road*."

Fitspur led them around a sharp turn. There before them stood a procession of idling yellow cabs, waiting to spill into the bustling streets of Trillium. Fitspur's rats zipped under them, unafraid of the huge metal vehicles that could crush them in seconds. They seemed to be sharing information with one another. The rat stationed at the front of the line, closest to the open door leading to the street, raced over to another, chattered with him a bit, and then that one went to the next rat, and so on, creating a chain of information.

Juniper was astonished by the flurry of activity before him. He'd seen Topside rats before—that was not unusual—but the sheer number before him was staggering. Across the way, on the opposite curb, a line of rats waited patiently in the shadows. There were no fewer than fifty, possibly more. He nudged Fitspur. "How many of you live Topside?"

Fitspur cocked his head and began counting on his claws. "Well sir, let's see. I transport hundreds weekly. Mind you, many are repeat customers, and mind you again, many city rats have no need to travel, quite happy where they are, especially with my customers visiting them on a regular basis from all over our fine city. And this is not the only operation, to be sure. We've got one in the Reserve and another on the city outskirts. So, all in all, I'd say our ranks lie somewhere in the tens of thousands—give or take a thousand or two, of course."

"Well . . . ," said Juniper, somewhat speechless, "I'm embarrassed to say I had no idea there were so many of you."

Chuckling, Fitspur whistled to a family of brown rats on the opposite curb, waving them to the front of the line. "Party for Brimstone Station, you're next!" He motioned to one of his assistants, who ushered them to a yellow cab, where they quickly disappeared into its undercarriage. "You groundlings live in your own world, oblivious to what goes on up here." He grinned.

"How do you stand it, though? Topside couldn't be more dangerous."

"And what's wrong with living dangerously?" said Fitspur, slapping Juniper on the back. "Keeps things interesting, if you ask me!" He nodded toward Billycan, who was explaining Fitspur's operation to the others. "That one used to come to me looking mad and disheveled. Saints only know what mischief he was up to—I didn't think it my business to ask. I just knew he was looking for others like him—his family. Why, sometimes he didn't even look like a rat, so wild he was."

"Where did he go?" asked Juniper curiously.

Fitspur lowered his voice. "He always seemed to end up back where he came from. You know, *that* horrible place."

"You mean . . . the lab?" whispered Juniper. "How did you know where it was?"

"I'm a city rat. We all knew where that horrible lab was." He shook his head. "I'd send that lad off, letting him ride around for hours under whichever car he liked—always searching for something, though I don't think he ever quite knew what that was. When I'd see him the next time, ask him where he'd been, it was always somewhere near the lab. With the wretched life he had there, you'd think he'd want to stay as far away as possible, but I suppose it was all he knew back then . . . his only real home."

"Yes," said Juniper, thinking about the scientists' diaries

and what Silvius claimed—that *everything* centered around the volcano, hidden somewhere in the museum.

The gray female raced up to Fitspur and nodded. "All right, then," he said, "your crew's next." He clapped his paws. "Quickly, everyone, or Saints only know how long you'll be stuck here waiting for another car headed that way. The museum closes soon!"

Billycan darted over to Fitspur as the others crossed the street. "Thank you once again for your help."

"I hope you find your friend," said Fitspur. "I hope you find everything you've been searching for all these years."

"I'll come back afterward and tell you all about it," said Billycan.

"Of course you will," said Fitspur, patting Billycan's shoulder. "Run along now, you'll miss your ride."

Billycan smiled faintly and dashed after the others.

"All right, pay attention now!" shouted the gray rat forcefully over the ruckus of the garage. "Everyone, underneath! Some of you may have done this before, so just consider this a refresher course!" She pointed to the undercarriage of the cab. "All of you climb in, on either side. Jump on, grab hold, and whatever you do, don't let go. It's going to be a rough ride!" The rats leaped up into the undercarriage as instructed. She specifically looked at Duncan and Oleander, who seemed more out of their element than the others. She pointed to a rounded silver box stuck in the center area of the undercarriage and a long metal tube feeding out of it. "That is the cab's muffler. Whatever you do, do *not* touch it. It will burn you to a crisp." Duncan grabbed his tail, pulling it as far away from the muffler's pipe as possible. "Do you all understand me?" Everyone nodded back at her.

"Good. When the doors to the cab open, you're at your stop—
Battery Park West at 79th. You can't miss the museum, biggest
building in sight, showy statues in front." The cab started to
roll. "Remember, don't let go . . . and good luck!" She dashed
back onto the curb and out of sight.

CHAPTER ELEVEN
Water Bound

HIS MIND AND HEART RACING, Billycan closed his eyes and took a deep breath as the cab tore down the street. Returning home, the salty smell of the Hellgate Sea had exhilarated him, but being in Trillium, his old hunting grounds, was electrifying. He thought of all those months he'd searched for any surviving albinos, trying to find anyone who might be family, when all along the rat who'd saved him from the fire in the lab and led him to safety was actually his mother. His heart suddenly sank in his chest. His mother, Lenore, had offered to take care of him—to look out for him in the Catacombs, to help him control his urge for violence—but thinking it was hopeless, he abandoned her, stealing away into the dark as she screamed out his name. He glanced at Juniper, wondering how different his life might have been had he taken her up on her offer. Maybe his mother *could* have made a difference, despite the power of the toxic chemicals pumping through his veins. He swallowed stiffly, thinking of the alternative . . . maybe not.

Billycan craned his neck, trying to catch the buildings as they zoomed by, but all he could see was a blur of stone and neon. He could smell the pigeons, the alley cats, even a bat or two, but then it hit him—the overwhelming smell of cooked meat. Beef, to be exact. His eyes rolled back slightly. He was ravenous. He'd caught a whiff of the City Steakhouse, an establishment almost as rich in history as the museum itself. He used to scavenge its alley, tearing through the trash bins and Dumpsters for scraps of meat and strips of gluey fat. He shook his head, trying to not think of food. At least he knew they were close. Yes, he could smell them—the chestnut carts, the aroma still lingering even at this late hour. "Be ready to jump, everyone," he called out over the drone of the engine. "We're here."

"Now!" yelled Juniper.

In unison the rats dropped from the car and leaped onto the curb the moment the wheels stopped. Never had they been in such an exposed space. Even Juniper stopped dead in his tracks, staring at the wide sidewalk that led to the vast museum. Toward the back of the museum he saw a tall stack, smoke pouring out of it. "Juniper!" shouted Cole, snapping him from his daze. "Move!"

With Billycan in the lead, they darted from the sidewalk onto the grass, hoping to be lost in the dark sea of green as they raced away from the sound of human feet. The moon was full and bright, bright enough to see nine rats tearing through the grass.

"I remember now!" shouted Duncan as they grew nearer to the colossal stone columns. He blew ahead of the others, his memories driving him. "This way!"

Two large statues sat on either side of the stairs leading up to the entrance, stone sentries dressed in antiquated military garb. Streaked a mossy green, each sentry waved his sword from atop a horse, its nostrils flared, ears back, ready to plunge into battle.

Duncan led them to the back of one of the statues. Panting, the rats gathered around, staring down through a metal grate at the base of the statue.

"Where does it lead?" asked Juniper.

Cringing a bit, knowing they would not like the answer, Duncan said, "It leads under the museum. That's how I got in the first time."

"Duncan," said Cole, "what are you *not* telling us?"

"Well, I . . . it's just that . . ."

Putting an ear to the grate, Juniper realized what Duncan was not telling them. "It leads to the sewer," said Juniper, patting Duncan's shoulder. He sighed. This was the last thing they needed. Memories of the Great Flood haunted the older rats, and nightmares terrorized the younger ones—so much had been lost. But with the doors of the museum locked tight for the night, everyone must face their fears.

Suttor made a face and moaned. "I'd rather go back to the swamp with all its snakes and poison plants than down there in the murk."

"Agreed," said Juniper, "but it may be our only option."

"Yes, it's how I found my way in the last time," said Duncan. "I don't want to go down there any more than the rest of you, but there's no other way in that I know of, at least not that I could find back then."

"If Victor got here before they closed, I'm sure he found a way inside," said Vincent. He knew his brother was more of a risk taker than he was. If he saw a way in, he would have taken it. "Even if some Topsiders spotted him, what would they have done?"

"Ignored him," said Suttor. "What's one lone pest slipping past them? Even if they did manage to alert someone at the museum, what would happen then? They're not going to waste time chasing after a rat loose in a place that size."

"I just hope he made it here," said Vincent.

Studying the hole in the grate, Billycan mentally sized up each rat. Duncan was by far the largest, but even he'd be able to squeeze through. "We don't have time to speculate." He glanced at Vincent. "Your brother took on *Killdeer*. I'm sure he made it here and figured out a way inside. There's something to be said for sheer grit."

Vincent studied Billycan's profile, finding it more than a little odd to agree with him on *anything*, but he spoke the truth. Whether it was justice for their dead family, a stolen moment with Petra, or now to find the lost Hunters, Victor was dogged when he wanted something.

Billycan looked over his shoulder at the faces of the Nightshade rats, each one consumed with dread of a watery doom. He had never feared water. "If Duncan can guide me, I'll take the lead," he said, turning his attention back to the grate. He'd swum in the Hellgate Sea and was quite sure he could handle the city sewer. "The ghosts of the Great Flood may still haunt you, but we rats are natural-born swimmers. You'll see."

As Juniper and Cole lined up the others, Vincent watched Billycan. A tremor traveled up the white rat's spine, causing his whole body to shudder. Billycan's mouth opened, baring his teeth. His eyes burst with color, their blood-red hue something Vincent had not seen since back in the swamp. Billycan turned back to the others, his eyes shifting back to the same muted red they'd been since he'd returned to Nightshade.

* * *

"It's all right!" Billycan shouted up to the others, his voice echoing against the sewer walls. Retching, he spat out a mouthful of dirty water. "Disgusting, but all right."

He looked around, his eyes adjusting to the dark. It was a large cylindrical tunnel made of bricks. He paddled over to water's edge. By the looks of it, this was an older part of the city's sewer system, probably not used in some time. The water was stagnant, covered with dead insects and bits of floating trash. It was deep, but if they stayed along the side of the tunnel, they'd only get their feet and tails wet—once they dried off from the initial plunge through the grate, at any rate.

Rat after rat tumbled gracelessly into the water, each one slightly stunned and gasping for breath as they broke the surface. Oleander seemed at home, though, hitting the water headfirst in an elegant, twisting dive. Having lived in the swamp all her life, water—polluted or otherwise—felt like home. The stench didn't bother her much, either. The odor of the fetid water was familiar, almost welcoming. She laughed as Carn choked and wheezed, sticking his tongue out in disgust. He spewed a mouthful of dirty water into the air, clumsily making his way to the edge.

"What's so funny?" he asked peevishly, wiping his mouth.

"Oh, nothing," she replied, with a familiar twinkle in her eye, "but if you start drowning, I'll be sure to rescue you."

"I can swim!" he said.

She giggled and pushed his shoulder. "Whatever you say, *Corn*."

He couldn't help but grin. Rats were natural swimmers, but he was clumsy in the water. "Don't start *that* again. I was just beginning to live down the legend of Corn the Snake Killer."

"You'll never live that down," said Suttor, lending him his paw and pulling him onto the narrow shoreline.

Duncan plunged into the water, slapping the surface with an impressive belly flop, splashing everyone. "Sorry," he said, shaking his head free of water.

"I just dried off!" protested Suttor, wiping the water from his whiskers.

"Ignore your brother's grousing," said Cole. "We'd never have found a way inside without you."

Juniper crouched on the shoreline, wringing water from his cloak. "We best get on our way. If Victor did make it inside, we need to find him before he gets himself into trouble."

"Trouble does seem to find my brother," said Vincent.

"That's what I'm afraid of."

They traveled down the winding sewer tunnel for about an hour. Oleander stayed at the back of the line. As the fastest swimmer, she could quickly dive in and save any rat who might accidentally fall in and need help. Clover, the least capable swimmer, walked in front of her. Juniper wanted his niece near Oleander, just in case.

Clover glanced over her shoulder and then up at the ceiling as odd, echoing howls swept over their heads and crept up from behind them. "Duncan," she asked uneasily, "how much farther?"

"There's an old stone staircase," he replied, pointing in front of him, "just around the turn a few yards ahead. It leads up into

the museum." He smiled. "I remember that the door opened up to the back of the caveman exhibit. I squeezed under the gap and there was a hairy Topsider foot right in front of me! I thought I was done for until I realized it was just a statue."

Glancing down at the murky water, Clover stopped short, causing Oleander to jerk back. "Sorry," she said, squinting through the dark. "I thought I saw something."

"Don't fret," Oleander replied, patting Clover's shoulder. "Back in the swamp, there's always something lurking in the water. The snakes have kept their word and stayed out of our territory, but still we're always on our guard. Luckily we have Dresden and his colony. The bats patrol our grounds regularly." She looked at the back of Billycan's head, a ghostly white blur at the front of the line. "I hate to admit it, but he really *has* changed, hasn't he?"

"Well," whispered Clover, "Billycan could have let Hecate and her cohorts kill us all, but he didn't. If he's got something else planned for us, he's surely taking his own sweet time—"

Before Clover could finish, the tunnel swiftly filled with a bloodcurdling scream, followed by a splash. "Oleander!" shouted Clover, whipping around.

She was gone.

"Oleander!" she yelled again into the dark. A choked shriek came from the water, followed by thrashing and then silence.

"Everyone, stay together!" commanded Cole.

Juniper tossed his satchel and cloak to the ground and dived into the water along with Billycan and Vincent. Carn was about to dive in, but Cole blocked his path. "No, Carn. Let them go."

"I've got to help them. It's Oleander! I can't leave her to die!"

"Vincent's a proven swimmer," Cole reminded him. "He and Victor made it through the Great Flood. Besides, you're too close to her. Your emotions might very well get in the way, and that could get someone killed." Carn nodded his head in miserable agreement. He knew Cole was right.

Vincent shouted for Oleander in between dives under the surface. "I can't find even a trace of her," he said as he came up for air a third time. "It's too dark! It's like she's vanished!"

"We'll find her," said Billycan. He sucked in another deep breath and plunged back into the gloom. Trillium rats had advanced nocturnal vision, but even he could make out little in the gloom. He dived to the bottom of the sewer, clawing through the thick sand, pulling himself through the water. Where was Oleander? She was clever and quick. She didn't just fall in, something, or someone, had her. But who—or what?

He swam toward the far wall of the sewer, looking for any trace of her. Feeling the cold bricks under his digits, he stumbled upon a narrow break in the wall, something no one would have noticed in the dark. It was a slender entrance, leading into another part of the sewer. She *had* to be there. He heaved himself up to the surface. "Juniper, Vincent, this way!"

Clutching his dagger between his teeth, Vincent couldn't help but think of his family as he made his way across the sewer. How strange life had become, he thought as he bulleted toward Billycan, *willingly* following after the rat who had caused his family's demise. What an extraordinary plan the Saints had set before them. But where might it end?

Billycan put a claw to his lips as Juniper and Vincent entered through the narrow passageway. He mouthed the word *listen* and pointed down the tunnel.

Their ears perked at the sound of breathing—deep, heavy pants that sounded not like a rat but something else entirely, something wild and violent, something that might rip your heart out.

With no shoreline to cling to, they slowly waded through the water, making their way closer to the breathing. That was when Vincent smelled it—the scent. He knew that scent! It had changed, there was something strained and desperate about it, something feral . . . but he knew it.

A cutting pain sliced through his leg, tangling his thoughts. Dropping his dagger into the water, he grunted out loud, unable to keep quiet though the pain. Blood clouded the water. He shouted in agony as teeth plunged into his open wound. "It's got me!" He reached for the creature, pulling at its muzzle, trying to disengage its vise-like grip.

Juniper and Billycan pitched themselves at the creature, ripping at it with teeth and claws, desperately trying to pull it off Vincent. They couldn't see the assailant, but they could feel it. Its jaw was long and lean, its wet fur thin and wiry, and though it was skeletally thin, its strength challenged their own, hard muscle covering its bones.

Unable to pull the creature off Vincent, Billycan dived underneath it, doing the one thing he knew might loosen its grip. He bared his teeth, forcing them with every ounce of strength deep into the base of the creature's tail, ripping it out of its socket. The creature flailed, thrashing through the bloodied water as it finally released Vincent's leg. Its head broke the surface, an agonized wail pouring from its mouth.

Fighting against the pain, Vincent dived to the bottom of the sewer, feeling for his dagger. He found the hilt of it in the sand. Grabbing it, he groaned as he launched himself back up. He reached for the creature as it struggled with Billycan on the surface. He took his dagger and thrust it into its belly.

Juniper grabbed it by its neck, slamming it into the brick wall. "Where is the girl?" he demanded. "What have you done with her?" Again he threw the writhing creature's head against the wall. "Answer me!"

"What makes you think I'll tell you, *Juniper*?" it hissed.

"How do you know my name?" The creature laughed wildly. With a final slam against the wall, it stopped moving long enough for Juniper to catch a glimpse of its face. He gasped. It was a rat—and not just any rat, but one he knew! It was one of the lost Hunters. "Topher?" he said, staring at his bulging eyes. The rat laughed psychotically, his whole body quaking with amusement. Juniper shook him by the shoulders. "Topher, what has happened? Why are you here? Have you been here all this time?"

"Time," repeated Topher, his eyes darting erratically. "Time, time, time, it means nothing, you know, nothing at all." He spat out a mouthful of blood—possibly Vincent's, possibly his own.

"Topher, please, tell me what happened when you left Nightshade."

"Nightshade, Nightshade, so many moons ago . . . so many moons . . ." muttered Topher.

"Where's Oleander?" asked Juniper. "What did you do with her?"

"Ohhhh, the pretty, pretty brown rat . . . the one I stole, the one I took." Topher smiled coyly. "So very pretty she was."

"Yes, the pretty brown rat," said Billycan, dragging Vincent over to the wall where a brick had broken, given him something to hang on to. "Where is she?"

"You!" said Topher, his hollow eyes widening. "You're one of them—from inside—aren't you?" Topher looked up at the ceiling, as though motioning to the museum over their heads. "You come from inside, like the others!"

"You mean from inside the museum?"

"Of course, from inside. There were many of you . . . you furry white devils."

Billycan exchanged glances with Juniper. "Topher, is there a lab inside the museum? Is that where you were?"

"Yes! Yes!" replied Topher excitedly, as though he'd just remembered. "How did you know? The lab!"

"Who brought you there?" asked Juniper. "Can you tell me?" Topher's eyes fluttered, rolling back in his head. He seemed to be growing weaker, his body growing heavier in Juniper's grasp. He was fading, losing blood fast. "Please think. *Who* brought you to the lab?"

"We were in an alley." Topher began to drool. His head swayed back and forth. "We saw food, fresh, beautiful food, meat, cheese, even candy—all there in the alley, of all places, ripe for the picking!"

"And what happened?"

Topher laughed again, but it was a wounded laugh, a laugh that transformed into a slow, mournful whimper. "I don't know." Tears streamed down his face. "I don't know. We were arguing over it, so odd, so very odd to see food like that in an alley. Then they took us." He looked up. "They took us inside."

"You mean inside the lab?" asked Juniper. Topher nodded. "Think hard, now. Tell me what happened in the lab."

Topher's voice dropped to an anguished whisper. "Unspeakable things . . . dreadful, horrible, unspeakable things." He let out a ragged breath. "There were needles . . . many, many needles. Many, many rats, dead rats, bodies taken every day, on a trolley." His eyes rolled back again. "Bleach . . . always, always the smell of bleach."

The word—bleach—caused something to ignite within Billycan. His body quaked with rage. Vincent watched as his eyes shifted, nearly glowing in the dark. Billycan gnashed his teeth, his rage building. It was all happening again. Silvius was right. The humans, they still wanted something from the rats, and would stop at nothing to find it. All his fears, his pain, the many years of agony in the lab resurfaced—the night when he met his mother, Lenore, the night he attacked the two men in the alley, saving her from their cages. How he longed to be back in that moment, slashing their foul, wrinkled faces all over again, showing them that they had no power over him *or* his kind. He panted in the water, his blood burning through his veins.

"It's all right," Vincent whispered. He set a paw on Billycan's shoulder. "It's all right. We're here now. We can stop them once and for all."

"Topher, where are the other Hunters?" asked Juniper.

"Oh, dead, dead as doornails," said Topher indifferently. "All dead, I reason—except for Liam. He escaped with me. He escaped. Liam escaped."

"Where is Liam now?"

Feebly, Topher motioned down the passageway with his snout. "With the pretty brown rat. The pretty brown . . ." He coughed up more blood, his wandering gaze finally catching Vincent's. "Your leg . . ." He laughed softly. "Sorry . . . so sorry. I bit you, did I? I think I'm sorry for that, at any rate. Did I bite you? Should I be sorry?" His eyes began to close.

"You've nothing to be sorry for," said Vincent. "You didn't know." His throat tightened as he spoke.

Topher's voice dropped to a barely audible murmur. "No, I didn't know. Maybe I knew . . . perhaps I knew." He smiled a peaceful smile. "I'm just . . . not sure. The Saints know . . . they always know." He let out a long breath and then fell silent.

"We have to leave him here for now," said Juniper. Trying to keep his composure, he released Topher's body, letting it sink silently into the water. "Saints be with you, friend. We will be back for you. I swear it."

"We must find this Liam before it's too late," said Billycan.

"Vincent, can you make it?" asked Juniper.

"Don't worry about me. It's the same leg that nearly got crushed under Killdeer's throne—it's used to pain. His teeth went deep, but he didn't hit the bone." He let go of the wall and began to swim down the tunnel. "We've got to find her."

They came to a small shoreline in the narrow tunnel, formed with sand and debris. There were odd piles of objects lining the brick wall. There was a stack of broken green glass from bottles, a mound of dented tin cans, and a heap of mismatched bones.

"This must be where Topher lived," whispered Billycan, looking down at the chaotic tracks in the sand. "By the looks of it, barely surviving off whatever he could find in the floating trash."

"But where is Liam?" asked Vincent. "I can't make out a scent among all this garbage."

"There's no time to waste," said Juniper. "Liam," he called, "can you hear me? It's Juniper." He kicked a tin can against the bricks, trying to make as much noise as possible to draw out the rat. "We know you're here. We know you have the pretty brown rat. You best come out of the shadows. Whatever you're feeling right now, whatever anger or confusion you've been going through, it's on account of the injections you and Topher were given in the lab. We're here to help you . . . to bring you home to Nightshade, where you belong."

A gasp came from where the sand met the brick wall, and a dark blur of a figure moved behind the pile of glass. Vincent walked toward it slowly, his dagger at the ready. "Come out,

Liam. It's Vincent Nightshade. I don't want to hurt you, but I will if you insist on staying hidden."

As he neared the glass, he noticed some of it was smeared with blood. His heart started to race. "I can hear you breathing back there," he called out. He took another step and noticed a long tail and two brown feet. With his free paw he waved Billycan and Juniper nearer.

"Bless the Saints," said Juniper as he saw the pair of lifeless feet. "Liam, what have you done?"

Another gasp came from behind the glass, followed by sobbing.

"Oleander?" said Vincent, finally bringing himself to round the corner and look at the full form of the limp rat on the ground.

Oleander sat behind the glass, rocking on her heels, her body coiled into a small ball. She covered her head with her arms, a broken shard of bloodied glass next to her, one clutched in her paw, and another embedded in the dead rat's chest.

Vincent crouched next to her. "It's Vincent, Oleander." He handed his dagger to Juniper, gently forcing her rigid arms off her head. He opened her paw and took the shard of glass from it. Softly he lifted her head. "It's all right now. You're safe."

"You knew him?" she asked, sniffling. "His name . . . it was Liam?"

"He was one of the lost Hunters," said Juniper. "He and Topher, the one who snatched you, they escaped the museum. They'd been trapped in the lab."

"I—I *killed* him," said Oleander. "He came at me . . . said I looked like a rat in the lab, one he'd gotten in a quarrel with. I didn't know who he was, or else I never would have . . ." She glanced down at the bloodied glass sticking out of the sand. "I never killed anyone before. I don't think I can live with it."

"He and Topher were given injections in the lab," said Vincent. "Whatever it was, it turned them mad. You cannot blame yourself. Had you not protected yourself, there's no telling what he might have done to you. You are lucky to be alive."

"But still . . . I took his *life*."

Billycan crumpled onto the sand, staring at Liam's wilted, malnourished frame. "He was already dead," he said. "Whatever life he had, he left it in that lab. If anything, you freed him from a future of agony and confusion. You gave him peace."

Juniper glanced around, noticing a small stack of metal placards. He reached for one. It read TOSCAN POT, CIRCA 1750. Another read TRILLIUM CITY MAYOR TANNER HUFFINGTON, 1892. "Where did they get these?" He scratched his head. "Did they steal them from the museum?"

Oleander pointed to the wall where a brick had been removed, revealing a sizable hole. "It's a tunnel. I think it leads up to the museum. I was trying to escape the other rat . . . Topher, you called him. I was outrunning him, when Liam came upon me halfway up the tunnel and dragged me back down here. The placards were all over the tunnel, stuck into the damp earth."

"We must get the others," said Juniper. He gazed up into the black tunnel. "This route might lead us to the lab quicker."

Limping, Vincent walked over to the pile of tin cans and began rifling through them, ripping off any lids still attached to them.

"What are you doing?" asked Billycan.

Vincent nodded at Liam's body. He tossed a silver lid to Billycan. "Burying him."

"I'll go back and get Topher," said Juniper. "They should be buried together."

Vincent and Billycan began to dig.

CHAPTER TWELVE
The Museum

N O ONE UTTERED A WORD the long way up the meandering tunnel, which traveled this way and that, clearly formed without logical thought. Pondering the fate of Nightshade's lost Hunters, they were filled with dread over the horrors that might await them in the lab.

The tunnel led into a large, darkened chamber, an exhibit hall of some sort, with alcoves roped off by gold cords. "'Look, but don't touch,'" said Suttor, reading from a sign. "Where's the fun in that?"

"This room," said Oleander, stepping toward one of the roped-off compartments marked TRILLIUM HOUSE 1875, "it reminds me of the parlor in the manor . . . back in the swamp."

Billycan looked up at the faded settee, recalling the very one he'd sat on in the manor parlor, plotting his own brother's demise. "Must everything dredge up my memories today?" he muttered wearily. His ears perked. He glanced toward the archway leading to another part of the museum. "Do you hear that?"

"Music," said Clover.

"Classical music," said Oleander. "When I was little, we sometimes played it on the phonograph. We'd drag out the records when the rain kept us inside the manor. Thicket and Stono would dance to it." She smiled, thinking of them. "They love to dance . . . when they aren't beating the tar out of each other."

Carn squeezed her paw. "We'll see them soon. I promise."

Billycan's face suddenly dropped. His jaw fell and his shoulders slumped. "Yes . . . classical music. She's right," he said limply.

"What is it?" asked Juniper.

"I've heard that music . . . before," Billycan said as if in a trance. "In fact"—he held up a claw, waving it in time with the melody—"the record will skip right . . . now."

To everyone's surprise, the record did skip exactly when Billycan said it would.

"How did you *know*?" asked Vincent.

"One of the lab techs, he liked records," said Billycan. "Stored them in his briefcase. That song . . . it's one of his favorites."

Juniper tightened the strap on his waterlogged satchel. "I believe we've found our secret lab."

They followed the music to another hall within the museum, its walls covered with old portraits. THE LORDS OF TRILLIUM read the long, gilded sign over the door. "Duncan, isn't this where you said you heard other rats?" asked Vincent.

"Yes," said Duncan, staring up at the portrait of a stout Topsider named Edward Grimsby III. "I remember his face."

The music seemed to originate from a cast-iron grate at

the base of the wall, a vent of some sort. Juniper approached the grate. He could hear no sound other than music—no rats, no Topsiders. Unexpectedly a rush of air flew up through the vent, ruffling his fur and temporarily muting the sounds of violins, flutes, and clarinets. Along with the air came something else—the smell of rat. He wanted to laugh and cry at the same time. There were too many scents; the sheer number overwhelmed him. Some he thought he might know, most others he'd never encountered. If what Topher said was true, and there were numerous white rats in the lab, Juniper wondered if any of them could be related to Billycan. Humans bred animals over and over without regard. Since Billycan's father was unknown, many of the albinos could be his family one way or another.

"They're down here," Juniper announced. The others didn't look surprised. They had gathered by the vent, following the scents floating around them. The smell of the rats' fear was deep, thick, and bitter—an acidic wave of terror that only other animals could sense.

"The lab I was in was well above ground," said Billycan. "All these scents are coming from down below."

"How are we going to get down there?" asked Vincent, examining the vent's slick metal lining. "There's nothing to hold onto, and no telling how far down the vent goes."

"I'm not sure," replied Juniper.

"The golden ropes!" cried Duncan. "They're all over the museum, roping off the exhibits. They have those fancy metal clasps on the end; we can hook them together. Surely they'll hold the nine of us."

"Good thinking," said Cole, patting his son on the back.

"You have a knack for figuring out sticky situations," said Juniper. "It was you, Duncan, who told us to climb down the chicken wire in the chimneys of the Kill Army kitchens."

"I did?" asked Duncan.

"You don't remember?" asked Cole. Duncan shook his head. "Well, do you remember Lali cooking you creamed corn with bacon the day you shared that information about the army kitchens?"

"Oh! Now I remember," said Duncan. "That used to be one of my favorites, when I was little." His stomach grumbled. "I wish I had some right now."

"Food always triggers his memory," said Suttor.

"When we make it home, you can have creamed corn with bacon to your heart's content," said Juniper. "Why, I'll make it myself." He chuckled softly.

"Uncle, you'll burn Nightshade City to the ground," said Clover, trying to lighten the mood. "You can't even make porridge without starting a fire."

"Let Lali handle the cooking," advised Cole. "Duncan's mother surely has better odds than you of keeping Nightshade from disintegrating into a pile of bacon-scented ashes."

Duncan nodded. "Yes . . . if we come out of this alive, I'll help her make it myself."

After hooking the brass clasps of the golden ropes together, the rats threaded the rope through the lattice of the grate, securing the last clasp to a cast-iron strip on the grate itself. Not knowing how deep the vent ran, they'd used every possible rope they could find, chasing after Duncan as he raced through the halls of the museum, pointing out which rooms had roped-off exhibits, most unchanged from years ago.

One by one the rats sank their claws into the thick velvet of the ropes and climbed down the vent, the echoing symphony creating an eerie setting as they descended. Finally a dull glow illuminated the vent. Vincent's foot hit bottom, his claws

scratching the slick metal. "Everyone, quiet now," he whispered, jerking his foot off the metal. "Soft on your feet."

Helping each other, they silently dropped onto the floor of the vent, quickly filling the small space. A light flickered in the music-filled lab. The scent of anxious rats was now intense, the sound of breathing loud.

"I can hear them," blurted Duncan. "I can hear them breathing."

"Hush," hissed Suttor, quickly covering his brother's mouth. He whispered in his ear, "We don't know what condition these rats are in—they could be like Topher and Liam, happy to rip us to pieces. And there could be scores of humans down here, just waiting to snatch us up and shove their needles in our hides! Understand?"

Eyes wide, Duncan nodded. "Good lad," whispered Suttor. "Listen to me. I already thought you were dead once. I couldn't bear to go through that again. Just pay attention, all right?"

"All right," said Duncan softly.

Billycan grasped the thin metal bars of the grate and peered out into the underground chamber. He knew this type of grate. He knew it . . . only this time he was on the other side of it. As a child, he recalled staring at the grates day in and day out, wondering where they led, wondering if they were a way out. These weren't the old cast-iron grates like up in the museum. They were slick and modern.

Without hesitation he slipped his entire arm through the grate and began loosening one of its screws.

"What are you doing?" asked Juniper in a hushed voice. "We have no plan."

"Then stay here," said Billycan, placing the first screw on the floor of the vent. He pushed past the others, knelt down and reached for the lowest screw on the other side of the grate. "I, for one, am sick and tired of waiting."

"It's too risky to go in blind," said Juniper. "I don't want anyone killed!"

"Then I'll say it again: stay *here*." Billycan deftly removed another screw, gently placing it on the floor next to the other.

Juniper grabbed Billycan's shoulder, spinning him around. "This is not just *your* fight!"

Billycan turned back to his work and reached up, feeling for the third screw on the other side of the grate. He spoke in an unruffled tone. "In the Catacombs, and well before the Catacombs, I commanded an army. Other than your little insurrection, I always won. Always. I know the ways of warfare. I learned in the lab from my friend and teacher Dorf. Dorf died in that lab. At the time, I wanted to die with him. He was the closest thing I had to a father. They took my friend from me at a time when I needed him most. They left no trace of him, all of his memory erased by the suffocating smell of bleach."

Billycan removed the third screw, quietly setting it next to the others. "So, if you please, this *is* my fight." With only one screw left, Billycan softly swung the grate aside and looked down into the space below him. "There is no secret strategy with the humans—no crafty plan we can come up with. They catch us, we die. Whether they kill us on sight or we die from their torturous experiments, the answer is always the same." His eyes moved over the anxious faces of the others. "Let me check the lab first. I will be the guinea pig, so to speak. I'm going now. I'll signal you if it's all clear." He craned forward, ready to jump.

"Wait." Clover pushed forward in the cramped space and stepped in front of Billycan. "You may not care if you lose your life down there, but Julius cares." She looked up at Juniper. "Your brother cares." She took Billycan's large paw in her own. "I care, too. I've only just found you, Uncle. I don't want to lose you just yet."

"Uncle . . ." he repeated in a whisper. He studied her for a moment. "How can you be so forgiving, after all I've done?"

Clover's eyes wandered over Billycan's elongated spine and overgrown neck, made that way by the daily injections. "You were put through terrible horrors. Horrors none of us could ever imagine." She glanced through the bars of the grate and out into the shadowy lab, hearing the faint murmurs of the captured rats. "I know you can help them . . . not just now, but after they're free. That's when they'll need you most, and that's why you can't die down there."

Billycan looked down for a moment, trying to keep his composure. Then he looked up and smiled an impossibly confident smile. "I'll be sure to come back, then."

He gave everyone one last look and silently dropped into the lab.

CHAPTER THIRTEEN
Frankenstein's Lab

BILLYCAN CROUCHED UNDER A LOFTY WALL OF CAGES, the metallic clang of countless feet above his head. The air was thick with fear—a scent so palpable any rat with common sense would run for his life. The echoing voices of those awake overlapped, one on top of the other, an eerie amalgamation of treble and bass mixing with the music.

He crept to the edge of the wall of cages and looked out into the dim lab. It seemed endless, far larger than the one he'd lived in. There was a long row of cages down the middle of the lab, and against the wall were workstations covered with large monitors and keyboards. Against the opposing wall were more cages and an open entrance that led to another part of the lab. The space was modern, everything polished and new, the low hum of equipment purring below the music. Stepping out quietly, he looked up at the vent, visible from all sides of the lab. He had to move quickly. He looked up, noticing a row of windows yards above the cages, too high to be reached by rats *or* humans. It dawned on him. Not only had the humans built a new lab, they'd gone underground, hiding the allegedly bankrupt labs of Prince Pharmaceuticals from their own kind. What sinister work were they up to now, that they had to keep this place a secret?

Other scents began to emerge—familiar scents. Images of the swamp and the rundown chapel flooded his head. His nose twitched wildly. His hackles rose and his mouth watered, the fragile aroma driving him into agitation. He could never forget the mild mix of lemon balm and arrowroot . . . the scent of the big brown bat.

Clutching a metal pole anchored to the base of the wall of cages, he peered around each corner: no humans in sight. He raced across the lab toward the scent, weaving his way under the endless row of cages lest a rat spot him and start a noisy ruckus.

As the scent grew stronger, it evoked a memory of the swamp—Billycan's endless quest for tender bat flesh. He forced himself to recall that he no longer ate bats . . . well, not the ones from Trillium in any case.

His ears perked as he heard the fluttering of wings. Night was the time when bats fed, even in this sterile excuse for a home. The scent of fear waned as he neared the bats' manmade roosts. They were more practical than rats, less emotional. Billycan respected that.

There they were . . . gliding in tight circles inside a great plastic cage, chasing after large winged beetles blown in through a clear plastic tube at the side of the cage. He cringed at the crunching of insect shells, the sound pouring out from the symmetrically placed air holes in the cage.

Halting at the edge of the last row of rat cages, he watched intently. The bats were graceful creatures, deftly dodging one another, weaving through the synthetic trees, snatching up insects without needing to look at them, their flight guided by the inaudible pulse that only bats could detect. They were actually quite amazing, he thought. It seemed there *was* more to them than just a delectable meal. He watched a rather large fellow, bulky for even a Trillium bat, clip his wing on the branch of a tree and plummet to the ground. Perhaps they *were* nothing more than a tasty snack after all.

Shrouded by shadows, Billycan took his chance and dashed for the corner of the cage where the bat had fallen. The bat's face was dark brown, similar in shape to a rat's, but his nose was slightly pushed in and his long ears were set close to his eyes, looking almost like bat wings themselves.

Silently Billycan approached, slowly popping his head into the bat's line of vision. "Bat," he whispered. The bat didn't notice him; he shook his head, readying himself to take wing. Billycan raised his voice. "Bat!"

The creature suddenly turned, jolted by the vision of Billycan. He didn't scream or soar away; instead he dragged himself closer to the edge of the cage, trying to get a better look.

"Who are you?" asked the bat, mystified. He glanced up at the long rows of cages across the lab. "You escaped your cage, didn't you? You better leave quickly, before the man comes back."

"The man?"

"Yes, the man in the white coat. He's here late every night. You should know that by now."

"Bat, what's your name?"

Narrowing his eyes, the bat cocked his head, inspecting the oversized white rat with only a thin pane of plastic between them. He glanced back at the other bats, all occupied with their nightly feeding high above his head. "I'm Willow," he whispered nervously.

"How old are you?" asked Billycan, peering at his boyish face.

"Old enough to know you must be one dense rat, standing in plain sight in a lab run by humans."

Billycan chuckled at the response. "Point taken." He looked up at the other bats, still swooping and diving for their insect dinners. "How did you all get captured?" he asked, studying the cage for any visible escape routes.

"It was daytime. I was sleeping at home, in our roost. We all were." Willow sighed glumly, staring down at the silver tag clamped tightly around his leg, the number 77 etched into the metal. "I heard a noise and opened my eyes. Burning yellow smoke clouded my vision. I tried to fly away, but I was suddenly too weak, like I'd been hit in the chest. The smoke—it made us fall asleep. We woke up in a truck. The next day we were here."

"So you're not from Trillium, then?" asked Billycan.

"Well, we weren't born here—at least I wasn't, but many of our colony were." He smiled proudly. "The leader of our colony was. He's the reason we moved away from Trillium in the first place—he kept the farmers from killing us altogether."

"You and your colony live in a chapel, don't you?" asked Billycan.

"Yes!" replied Willow excitedly. "How did you know that?"

Before Billycan could reply, a bat plunged toward them at breakneck speed. It hurled its body into the plastic pane. Billycan jumped back as the bat grabbed Willow, pulling him away from the edge of the cage. "Don't you touch him!" it screamed bitterly. It was a female with a camel-colored coat and exceptionally large ears set close to her tiny black eyes.

"I mean no harm," said Billycan.

"No harm, indeed!" She spat at the pane. "How did you find us?" she demanded. "What are you doing here?"

Another bat swooped down, a sturdy male with a pushed-up nose that pointed skyward at a most severe angle. "Telula, Willow, stay back!"

"Don't worry, Cotton," said Telula.

Billycan held up his paws, trying to quiet them. "Please, keep your voices down. If you get me killed, all will be lost!"

"Oh, and we'd be so disappointed!" said Telula derisively. "By rights you should have died back in the swamp!"

"You have every reason not to believe me, but I'm here to help you." Billycan pointed toward the vent. "Look. Can you see them from here? There are Nightshade rats waiting in the vent, ready to come down at my signal."

"Is Juniper up there?" asked Cotton, squinting as he looked at the vent, now hanging slightly askew on the wall. "I see feet, or at least I think it's feet."

"Yes! Juniper is up there. Vincent, Carn, and Oleander, too."

"Don't believe him," said Telula, stepping between her brothers. "You may be Juniper's kin. And yes, we heard the news of your supposed cure from Oleander and Carn. But I'll gamble you're as wicked as ever!"

"What are you three going on about?" asked a stern voice from behind them. "Why, the whole colony can hear your bickering!"

"Father—"

"Hush, Telula," said the older bat.

Telula snarled in frustration, unfurling her wing in Billycan's direction. "Father, look!"

Slowly Dresden stepped forward. His eyes met Billycan's. He craned forward and studied him closely. He had never imagined he'd see the white rat again—the White Assassin, as they'd called him in the swamp. "Your eyes," he finally said, "they're different, subdued. I'd heard the reports—that you'd changed. Our brethren in Tosca, the Canyon Bats, they told me of you, of your good works since Silvius . . . well, *retired*."

"Father, you can't be serious!" said Telula, aghast. "You actually think his transformation is genuine?"

"Do you think the leader of the Canyon Bat Colony would lie?"

"Well . . . no," said Telula, "but it may be part of some elaborate plot. You know him—always scheming."

"You know Silvius?" asked Billycan.

"After he escaped from the lab, he lived on the outskirts of Trillium. He and a few other rats resided on the farmland we came from. We struck up an agreement, he and I. We kept watch for those pesky country cats, and of course the farmers, while Silvius and others helped keep owls away from our colony, scaling trees and destroying their nests—sometimes even fighting them on our behalf." Dresden shook his head. "I was saddened to hear the news of Silvius's dementia. He was always an ally to the bats. not to mention a dear friend."

"Father, even if what you say is true, how can you believe *him*?" asked Cotton. "Just a year ago he was dead set on wiping out our entire colony. What if it's all an act?"

"I receive reports from Juniper and the Council on a regular basis. The Colony Leader Summit was just last month, lest you forget, and who attended?"

"The Canyon Bats," said Telula softly.

"Yes, and they told me of Billycan's transformation. I would have flown to Trillium and told Juniper myself, had our capture not occurred."

"Well, that's still not proof enough for me," said Telula, sneering through the plastic pane.

Willow, stepping next to his father, said, "You were scary. The mere thought of you kept me from sleeping, back when you were in the swamp."

"I'm sorry for that," said Billycan. "I'm a different rat now."

"Let's hope," said Cotton skeptically.

"How did you find us?" asked Dresden.

"It's a long story," said Billycan, "but as we had suspected, the Topsiders are back at their *research*." He glanced around the lab. "We need to stop it—once and for all."

"On that we agree," said Telula.

Telula had every right to feel angry. All the bats did. Billycan looked up at them. They were all staring fixedly at him, hanging upside down on the artificial tree limbs, some quaking with fear, bits of guano dropping from the youngest. "Dresden, freedom is near. Juniper and the others are waiting up in the vent. Have you learned anything since your capture? Any idea what they're after?"

"All I can tell you is they're killing us off quickly, twenty of my colony gone already and at least triple that number of your kind." Dresden motioned to a long desk on which sat lab equipment and paperwork, a single row of cages pressed against the end of it. "I trust you remember Cobweb and Montague, your lieutenants back in the swamp? After we were captured, those brave rats jumped into the truck, trying to free us. Instead, they were captured too. One of the scientists seems to have taken a shine to them. They're locked up over there where he works—the only rats kept in that area. If anyone would know anything, it's them."

Slow, heavy footsteps grew closer. Billycan's body tensed. "We'll be back for you," he promised, and then darted across the lab.

* * *

Carefully he scaled the back of the long table, climbing up the electrical cords, a veritable jungle of wires and cables. He crawled behind a panel of monitors, all warm and glowing.

He ducked his head out from under the monitor flanking the row of cages Dresden had pointed out. Whoever had walked back into the lab had left again. Billycan looked at the row of cages, all empty except for the one nearest the table.

The cage was very much like the one he'd lived in for half his life. The closer he got to it, the more he felt like retreating. Inside the cage Cobweb and Montague huddled together in a far corner, each with a shiny silver tag strapped to his neck. Billycan sneered at the blue kibble in a small plastic dish; the scent still sickened him. He hurried up to the cage and shook the bars lightly. "Cobweb, Montague, wake up! Don't be alarmed." The rats did not rouse.

Hesitantly, Billycan reached for the latch. How he'd dreamed for years about being able to unlatch his own cage. He silently

lifted the pin and slid it out of the small metal holes that held it fast, smoothly unlocking the door—how easy it was!

Leaving the door partially open, he stepped tentatively inside. Cobweb and Montague did not stir. They looked thin, fragile, not the robust swamp rats he remembered, his two seconds-in-command. He knelt down and picked up a piece of the dry blue kibble, the synthetic food that had always left him feeling hungrier than before and made his stomach twist in agony. As he let the piece fall to the ground, the two gray rats finally stirred.

Montague's eyes opened. Blearily he looked right at Billycan. Within seconds he was up, no longer dreaming. He grabbed his sleeping brother by the chest, yanking him farther back into the corner of the cage. "Cobweb, wake up!"

Cobweb woke with a gasp, his eyes landing on Billycan. He stood in front of his brother and snarled. The two terrified rats brandished their claws and teeth. "You!" shouted Cobweb.

"Stay back!" shouted Montague.

Cobweb charged. Gritting his teeth, he growled and jumped up, kicking Billycan in the throat and knocking him against the cage wall.

Billycan lay on the ground, stunned. He grabbed the slim metal bars of the cage door. Coughing, he pulled himself back to his feet. "I . . . I suppose I deserve that, and more. But . . . I'm not here . . . to hurt you," he panted. Rubbing his throat, he pointed to the slender window on the side of the cage. "See for yourself. You're . . . close enough to see them from here. Look at the vent . . . on the wall". He fell to his knees, still struggling for breath. "Juniper . . . and the Council . . . they're up there, waiting to help you and the others escape."

Montague squinted up at the vent. "There are rats up there, to be sure. I can make out their forms."

"How do we know they're Nightshade rats?" asked Cobweb, glaring at Billycan. "They could be rats from his old regime."

Billycan got to his feet, still holding his throat. "Even if I'm lying, would it matter? Look around you. You are not in a position to be picky." He nodded to the cage door. "Besides, you're both free to go anytime you like. You can leave right now, if you choose."

The brothers exchanged glances. "We aren't cowards," said Montague. "We're not about to leave the others to die. We wouldn't do that."

Billycan looked at the monitors, all glowing a ghostly blue. "What happened to the other swamp rats? Are they here?"

"After the bats were removed, Oleander's father, Mannux, led the rats behind the manor and right into the chapel—hiding them in the only place the humans would never look for them, having just cleared the place of the bats."

"Clever move. What can you tell me of the lab? Do you know what's in the injections?"

"We know it's deadly," said Cobweb. "Most rats seem all right at first, but then they change, grow angry and bewildered . . . and very, very sick. Then they die. Rats that seem to be able to endure the injections and aren't driven mad, they just disappear. They're removed from the lab. We don't know where they go, but I suppose they're all dead too."

"We've been lucky so far," said Montague. "The chief scientist seems to like us. He hasn't given us any injections yet."

"It's strange," said Cobweb. "He's in charge of the entire laboratory, yet he seems intimidated by the men in suits."

"*Who?*" asked Billycan.

"His superiors," said Montague. "They come in dark suits, carrying briefcases—an army of them sometimes. They argue with Walter a lot, telling him the operation must move faster, threatening to take 'drastic measures' if he doesn't get the results they want."

Eyeing his surroundings, Billycan stepped out of the cage for a moment and looked at the stack of papers in front of the monitors. Each one read "Confidential, Intellectual Property of Prince Industries" in bold letters across the top. He remembered the men in the suits, always very grim and perpetually unhappy.

The classical music suddenly grew louder. "He's coming back," said Cobweb nervously. "This is his favorite part of the song. He always turns up the volume for this part!"

Billycan slipped back into the cage, moving to its darkest corner. "He mustn't see me," he said.

"Of course not," said Montague. "A third rat can't suddenly appear in our cage. That would certainly make him suspicious."

"That's not the only reason," said Billycan. He reached for his neck, feeling where his lab tag had been for so many years. "You see, he might remember me."

CHAPTER FOURTEEN
Walter

MUCH ROUNDER THAN BILLYCAN RECALLED, Walter shuffled back to his stool in front of the monitors, his short, stocky frame encased in a white lab coat. The scents of coffee and the dried liver he always kept in his pockets as treats wafted off him.

He'd grown old in the years since Billycan had last seen him. The brown hair that had lined the sides of his bald head was now a fluffy white, and the wrinkles around his eyes and mouth had grown deep and rutted.

So he's in charge now, thought Billycan, remembering that Walter was a mere lab tech all those years ago. He'd risen through the ranks, in a way much like Billycan.

Walter took a deep breath. He removed his spectacles and rubbed the bridge of his nose. His once rosy skin was slack and sallow. He closed his eyes, waving his pen in time with the music.

Walter sighed and put his glasses back on. He looked down

at the pile of papers before him. Reaching into his pocket, he dumped a handful of silver tags onto the table. He began scribbling their numbers on a piece of paper. "An additional twenty today . . ." Walter slammed down the pen. "At this rate, all our subjects will dead before we can fix the drug."

He pulled more tags from another pocket and placed them next to the others. They were like the small clasps Willow and his family had strapped around their legs. After counting them, Walter wrote down the numbers. "And seven bats today—that's a record." He got up and disappeared down a hallway.

"Where did he go?" asked Billycan.

"To get the cart," said Montague.

"The cart?"

"You'll see."

Walter quickly returned with a long metal cart. It had two trays on it, one on the top, another on the bottom. Cobweb quickly covered his nose. Billycan now knew what Topher had meant when he'd spoken of the trolley. The smell of death was overwhelming.

Twenty rats, stiff and cold, lay on the top tray. They were skin and bone. Nearly half were albino, the other half in various shades—probably the ones captured in Trillium City. Billycan couldn't bear to look at them.

His back to the cages, Walter stood in front of the cart. He looked down at his papers and began typing numbers on the keyboard in front of the monitors.

"Where does he take the cart?" whispered Billycan.

"We don't know," said Montague. "One thing's for certain, it always comes back empty. What does it matter? Let the man leave and we can open all the cages while he's gone."

"We have to do more than merely free everyone. If we don't, this will only happen again. We have to stop them *permanently.*

We need to go with him—to see every inch of this place. There could be more rats we don't know about."

"What if we're caught?" asked Cobweb.

Billycan looked up at the vent. Cobweb and Montague were in no condition to go with him. They were skeletally thin. Their coats were patchy and dull. Their eyes were bloodshot. "You two get Juniper and the others down here and start unlocking cages. We can't be sure how many humans are inside. Everybody must stay in their cages until we have an escape plan, understand?" They nodded. Billycan glanced at Walter, still busy with his paperwork. "I'll follow him."

"But what about those who are sick?" asked Montague. "They won't willingly stay in their cages. They've gone mad. They'll only cause chaos."

"Yes, of course," said Billycan, thinking of Topher and Liam. "They must be left here. There's no other choice."

"They'll die!"

"They've already been given a death sentence!" hissed Billycan. "We cannot help them." He crept out the door of the cage, gently shutting it. To the naked eye it still looked locked. "Stay put until we're gone." He slipped around the side of the row of cages and climbed down to the floor, using the wire windows as a ladder. He stole quickly past Walter's feet and stepped lightly onto the lower tray of the cart. Seven dead bats lay at his feet, their dark faces mirroring the shape of his own.

The cart began to move, slowly rolling down a dark hallway with a checkerboard floor. Walter stopped at an elevator, punching in numbers on a keypad affixed to the wall. The keypad beeped and the doors of the elevator opened. As they entered the small compartment, Walter took something from his breast pocket and put it over his face. It was a small white mask that covered his nose and mouth.

The elevator descended swiftly. Billycan's stomach dropped. They were already well under the museum. How far into the earth could they go?

When the doors of the elevator opened, they emerged into darkness, the only visible light a flashing red bulb in the distance. Walter pushed the cart down a narrow corridor that led to a set of metal doors highlighted by the pulsing red glow. He punched a code into another keypad on the wall and put on a pair of thick black gloves. The doors opened, sliding into the walls.

They entered a cave, sounds echoing all around them. An overwhelming smell filled Billycan's nostrils. It was oddly familiar, brackish, verging on rotten, but strangely it didn't bother him. In fact he suddenly felt more at ease.

Walter pushed the cart into an open area and left it there. He walked to a metal railing that ran around the central space. He placed his gloved hands on top of the railing and looked down.

Billycan jumped off the cart. The ground was warm under his feet. He padded behind Walter, hiding himself beneath the railing.

He looked down, then clutched the railing and jerked his body back, stunned by the sight below him—a vast, cavernous hole in the earth! From the center of the hole jutted a lofty rock formation, a small mountain. Billycan stifled a gasp. The volcano!

Billycan sniffed the air, realizing the moldering scent grew stronger the nearer he was to the rock formation. "Brimstone," whispered a voice from behind him.

He whipped around, mechanically priming his claws for a fight. He lurched forward, about to strike, but stopped short when he saw the black rat before him. Billycan grabbed him by the shoulders. "Victor! You're all right?"

Victor's eyes darted around the cave. "Yes," he whispered nervously, "I think so."

"How did you get here?"

"I followed Duncan's directions through the sewer and up into the museum. I heard music and was going to follow it, but found a rat-made tunnel instead. It led me right to the lab. I tried to catch a scent in the tunnel, but all I could smell was chemicals." He rubbed between his eyes. "I followed one of the scientists down here, but got locked inside."

"The blue kibble the scientists feed the rats," said Billycan. "That's what you smelled in the tunnel. Its artificial scent seems to take over everything." Victor seemed quite shaken, so much so that Billycan decided not to mention that Topher and Liam had made the tunnel. Victor need not hear what had happened to the Hunters just yet. If he only knew how lucky he was not to have come across them alone in the sewer!

"What you said just now, *brimstone*. What did you mean?" asked Billycan. "That's Trillium City's original name, from the old days."

"The diary Juniper and Cole found in the museum archives last year said we lived in the core of the extinct volcano for hundreds of years. We were isolated, trapped in our own little world, unaffected by the elements outside. It wasn't until the scientists discovered us that we found out we were so far advanced compared to other rats." He stared down at the mountain. "The diary spoke of a mineral on the shores of the Hellgate Sea, a remnant of the volcano."

"Brimstone?" asked Billycan. Victor nodded. "Maybe that's what we've been chasing all this time, going to the swamp and

Tosca—but their volcanoes were exposed. The elements must have carried away the brimstone."

Walter turned. "Hurry," said Billycan. "Onto the cart." They dashed back to the cart, leaping onto the lower tray before Walter could spot them.

At the sight of the seven lifeless bats, Victor nearly ruined their cover. Stumbling over the feet of a dead bat, he crawled frantically backward in a crab walk into the corner of the tray, the weight of his body nearly toppling it. Billycan promptly took him by the scruff of the neck and yanked him toward the center of the tray, evening out their weight. "Steady, now," he said, releasing his grasp. "You're all right."

"How did you stand it?" Victor asked bleakly.

"You mean the lab?" Victor nodded. "I'm not sure," said Billycan. "It was the only life I knew back then. I suppose one can grow accustomed to anything."

"I'm sorry," said Victor.

"For what?"

"For what happened to you. I didn't understand what you went through until I saw for myself what they were doing to the rats. I was only in the lab a short while, and I saw more than I could stomach for a lifetime."

"And what did you see?" asked Billycan.

"I've seen so much horror in the few hours I've been here! Starving rats begging for food, banging around their cages, their minds eaten away, their eyes hollow and sunken. I saw the humans jab them with needles filled with a thick black fluid. Then they took their blood, testing it in their equipment, writing down the results, and then tossing it away into a yellow can as though it meant nothing to them!"

"It *doesn't* mean anything to them," said Billycan, inspecting the row of dead bats, who all looked very young.

They were going down a ramp. "There are *more* of them down there," whispered Victor.

The astringent scent of perspiring humans filled the air, mingling with the smell of the brimstone. A man walked up the ramp as Walter came down with the cart. The man was in a blue one-piece garment. He had large round goggles covering his eyes, a black mask over his nose and mouth, a hard hat, and oversized earmuffs to protect his hearing, giving him the look of a giant insect. He pulled down his mask. He was dirty, his face covered in sweat and ash. He and Walter stopped for a moment and exchanged words.

"Going to the Clean Room?" asked the man.

Walter nodded, pulling down his face mask. "After I deal with these," he said, glancing at the cart.

"I still don't understand why you insist on tossing them yourself," said the man. "You've got lackeys for that, you know." The man waved him off before Walter could respond. "I know. I know. You respect your subjects for giving their life to science."

"What's the latest?" asked Walter, nodding toward the volcano.

The man removed his earmuffs, resting them around his neck. "Well, we set off the explosion in the right quadrant, just like you directed. Given the uncertainty of the volcanic plug, we used only a small amount of explosives, but it was enough to open things up."

"Anything?"

The man shrugged. "Just more petrified stone—no live magma." He nodded at the rock formation. "This thing's as dead as those rats, Doctor. The stone's much darker, though, if that means anything."

"If we find active magma, the mineral deposits will be far more potent—the darker stone is a good sign. It should be much easier to isolate the mineral now," said Walter, patting the man's shoulder. "Think of the bonus we'll all get if we're successful. Can you imagine? None of us will ever have to work again."

The man laughed. "My grandchildren and their children's children will never have to work again either. You make a good point." He started up the ramp. "I guess that's why you make the big bucks, huh, Doc?"

Walter didn't answer. He simply nodded with a closed-lip smile and continued down the ramp.

They passed several other men, all dressed in the same hard hats and blue jumpsuits. They were digging at the base of the rock. It was obvious where the explosion had taken place; large chunks of gray earth had been blasted away, revealing lustrous black rock beneath. The men were chipping away at the black rock, dumping it into wheelbarrows and moving down a corridor with them. They returned with empty barrows and then repeated the process.

"Victor, you said the needles, they were filled with a black substance?"

"Black as night," said Victor.

Billycan looked down at the bats again, struck by their youthful faces. What must it be like to die so young? "What do you notice about these bats . . . other than the obvious, of course?" he asked Victor.

Victor swallowed hard, steeling himself. He looked down at the still row of bats. After a moment he cocked his head in thought. "They . . . they're all children," he said.

"And large children at that," added Billycan. "Where are they coming from? The colony's children are a fine size, but these pups are as large as full-grown bats."

*   *   *

Walter wheeled the cart the rest of the way down the ramp and onto a stone walkway about the width of a city sidewalk. After circling halfway around the tower of rock, they came to a heavy iron door.

Walter entered the security code. The bolt inside the door clicked and the door popped open just a crack. Letting go of the cart, Walter pulled open the weighty door and rolled the cart inside, locking the door behind him.

The room was empty except for a large steel contraption in the center. The silver machine consisted of a long metal box with a barrel protruding from its side. Giant metal tubes shot out from the barrel like a man-made tree, leading all the way up to the cavernous ceiling.

The machine vibrated with sound. Heat radiated from it, making the air ripple. Walter wiped his brow, put on a pair of protective goggles, and wheeled the cart toward the machine.

"C'mon," said Billycan, "we must get off the cart—now!"

Billycan jumped off the back of the cart between Walter's legs, and Victor followed, just grazing a trouser leg. Walter looked down for a moment, then continued toward the machine.

"What's happening?" asked Victor as they dashed behind a steel beam.

"I don't think you want to know," said Billycan.

Victor heard a rush of sound, and a gust of hot air swirled around the beam. "No, I need to watch this."

In silence the two rats stood on either side of the beam and watched as twenty rats and seven bats were picked up one by one with a pair of rusty pincers and tossed into the fire-breathing coffer, their bodies quickly turning to ash, every trace of them incinerated.

CHAPTER FIFTEEN
The Clean Room

WALTER LEFT THE CART BEHIND, so Victor and Billycan followed him on foot. Other than the well-lit area where the men were digging, the cave was drenched in shadows and full of outcroppings, making it easy for them to stay unseen.

Walter made his way back to the stone walkway and followed it around the other side of the rock formation. He stared up at it for a moment, sighed wistfully, and headed down another corridor.

The corridor led to a small glass room lined with metal cubbyholes and hooks. As the doors opened, the rats sprinted into one of the cubbyholes nearest the floor and watched as Walter took off his lab coat and hung it on a hook. He then emptied his pockets and placed their contents in an empty cubby.

Walter took something from inside a wide metal box attached to the wall. He sat down on a long bench below it. At first it looked like he was holding two crumpled tissues, but then he stretched them out, crossed one leg over the other, grunting as he did so, and placed one of the stretched tissues over his shoe—a protective covering of some sort. After covering both shoes, he slowly stood up and walked over to a long steel rack where several paper-thin white garments hung. He took one and put it on. It was similar to the blue jumpsuits the other men had on, only it was exceptionally clean—not even a lone piece of lint. He zipped the suit up to his chin, then reached into a plastic bag attached to the hanger and took out a white mask and matching hat. The mask covered his nose and mouth, and the hat covered his entire forehead with a flap in the back that covered his neck and curled around either side of his head all the way to his ears. Once everything was snapped in place, only Walter's blue eyes were visible. Last but not least, he put on a pair of latex gloves and plastic goggles.

He walked to a set of glass doors on the other side of the room. He didn't press a keypad this time; instead he pressed a red button and said his name, "Walter Lee Harris." A loud buzzer sounded, and then there was the decisive snap of doors unlocking.

"Hurry!" hissed Billycan as Walter reached for a handle. "We can't lose him now." The rats dashed from the cubby and skittered across the tile in a panic. Walter pulled open the heavy doors and stepped inside the next chamber. As the doors began to close, Billycan hurled his body toward the opening. He slid on his back through the doors, quickly turning in time to see Victor skidding across the tile and through the small opening. He looked to be safely through, but his tail caught under one of the doors. His face flooded with terror, Victor yanked on his tail, but it would not break free. Swiftly Billycan grabbed him around the neck and jerked his body back as hard as he could, just before the doors slammed shut.

Victor winced in pain, grimacing at his freshly skinned tail, as he and Billycan picked themselves off the floor. They scanned the small room, looking for a place to hide. The room was brightly lit, with nothing in it except the white tile floor. Suddenly Billycan pointed to the wall. Round silver containers lined it symmetrically, each one about the size of a coffee can. They dashed into one of the lowest containers and waited for Walter to make his next move. The container was made of slick metal, and the back was dotted with long thin holes all the same size. Billycan peered around the lip of the container, only to see Walter standing in place.

"What's he doing?" whispered Victor.

"I don't know . . . he's just standing there."

All of a sudden a deafening buzzer sounded, followed by an explosive torrent of air bursting from the holes in the back of the container. "Grab hold!" shouted Victor as Billycan frantically pulled himself back inside.

They sank their claws into the holes, bracing their bodies as best they could as the air rushed past them. Not having enough time to get a solid hold, Billycan began to lose his grip. His left paw broke free and he was blown out into the room, his right paw desperately clinging to the lip of the container.

"Hang on!" shouted Victor over the noise. He shoved his claws farther into the metal holes, causing the beds of his nails to bleed. With his right paw he reached for Billycan, just able to grab hold of his paw that still gripped the container. Forcing his body to move against the air, Victor slowly turned around, planting his heels against the lip of the container. He held onto Billycan, determined to pull him back inside.

All at once the flood of air stopped. With Victor still pulling him, Billycan tumbled back into the container, slamming into

the back of it. He groaned for a moment, his head ringing with pain. "Walter . . . we must follow him. . . . ," he finally said.

Victor poked his head out of the container and saw Walter pushing through another set of doors. Without thinking, Victor seized Billycan under his arms and yanked him out of the hole, heaving him to the ground.

They landed in a heap on the tile. His wits returning, Billycan stumbled to his feet. "Go!" he screamed.

They were in a sort of glass box. Everything was silver or white, and gleaming, not even a fingerprint marring a surface. "This must be the Clean Room," said Billycan, "the place the other man mentioned."

"What was the other room?" whispered Victor, examining a bleeding claw. "I thought my skin would be ripped from my bones!"

Billycan shrugged. "I suppose that's how they get you clean."

They hid with little difficulty, ducking under steel desks,

chairs, and droning machinery, remaining unseen as they chased after Walter.

Every few steps he'd check in with someone, presumably his team of scientists, all dressed in the same white outfits, making them look like ghosts—every one of them bent over a microscope or running a vial through one machine and then placing it inside another, all busy at work.

Toward the end of the chamber was a metal counter, which ran around a tall glass dome. Walter stopped in front of it and looked inside. He tilted his head and looked down into the dome.

A female scientist walked up to him. "Dr. Harris, the new stone, it's everything we thought it would be and more! It was just like you said. The mineral deposits are richer, much easier to isolate. In only two days, the results are astounding."

"I can see that," said Walter, looking down into the dome. "Quite an amazing discovery. Dr. Sheppard, tell me—with our new findings, do we have any chance of meeting Prince's expectations?"

"Oh, Dr. Harris, you mean no one's told you?" She giggled, thrilled to have such an honor. "The deeper the miners get into the rock, the higher the mineral count. Not only will we meet their expectations, we'll far exceed them! Our findings will change the world as we know it." She sighed with satisfaction. "Your idea—the explosion—was genius, Doctor." She stared up at him, her eyes filled with admiration.

"Thank you, Dr. Sheppard," he said.

"Of course, sir," she replied.

Walter continued to stare into the dome, his eyes flat.

Victor looked around. All the scientists were busy with their work. "Billycan, c'mon, let's find out what he's looking at."

"Are you insane?" said Billycan. "It's not safe, there are humans everywhere."

Victor tilted his head. "Since when are *you* scared of humans . . . or anyone, for that matter?"

Exhaling, Billycan looked up at the looming dome. Even in the sterile Clean Room, the smell of rats was all around him, but something about the scent was off. "Truth be told, I don't want to find out what lurks inside that dome." He turned his face away from Victor. "I don't want to see the perversions of our species that they've created. For the life of me, I cannot stomach it." His paws started to tremble. His head throbbed, the rage inside him pounding, ready to burst. Walter might have been nice to him in the lab, but at that moment all he wanted to do was dig his claws into his fleshy skin, climb up his sagging body, and rip his eyes out. "I'm afraid"—he took a deep breath—"I'm afraid I'll do something . . . *unkind.*"

"Let me see your face!" said Victor.

Billycan turned his gaze toward Victor, his eyes a cruel, radiant red.

"I knew it!" said Victor. "The night of Vincent and Clover's wedding, when you screamed at me in the morgue . . . your eyes . . . they changed. They looked like they do now."

"I didn't want to react like that," said Billycan. "Sometimes a feeling comes over me, a feeling I cannot explain. Rats like Hecate bring it out in me. Or humans like him . . ." His eyes shifted up toward Walter. "Looking at him, it's hard to feel anything but hatred. It eats away at me."

"It's the same feeling you always felt before Juniper gave you the cure, isn't it—bloodlust?"

Billycan nodded. "It was you, wasn't it? Back in Nightshade, that night after my episode in the morgue. It was you at the top of the stairs. I smelled you. I was sure of it."

"I followed you."

"So you saw what I'd done in the corridor. I didn't remember any of it, but still I knew I had done the damage."

"I didn't see you do it, but I saw the end result. So you can't control it?"

"At first, after the cure, I thought I could . . . but lately it seems to be controlling me." He looked at his yellow claws, wondering about the exact number of lives they'd taken. "The Cortexa, the cure I was given, I don't think it's permanent. Sometimes . . . I want to hurt someone. I want them to feel pain. I dream about killing. If Texi hadn't got to Hecate first, I would have found a way to do it myself. I was already plotting her demise. He shuddered. "I fear I might change back to the way I was before at any moment. I'm worried I might kill someone . . . with no way to stop myself."

"Maybe it's time to face your fears."

"What do you mean?"

"When the man burned those rats' bodies to ashes, I forced myself to watch because I knew if I did, I could never turn my back on them. Maybe if you see what's in that dome you'll realize that ending this once and for all is more important than slashing some chubby old scientist's throat."

Billycan smiled. "You're awfully smart for a rat your age. Did Juniper teach you to think like that?"

"No," said Victor, "my brother did."

Walter had left the dome and gone to one of the many workstations, where he was poring over his team's new findings. The two rats crept around the dome to the area farthest away from the scientists. They jumped onto the circular table, the noise from the many machines drowning out the sound of their claws scraping metal.

They stood up on their hind legs and stretched their bodies

as far as they would go, trying to see over the steel base surrounding the dome.

What they saw was perplexing—rats of every conceivable color, all of brute size, as big as Billycan, and they were all young. Some wrestled playfully in the shavings on the bottom of the dome. Some curled together, crawling on top of each other as juvenile rats tended to do. They were running in and out of plastic tubes and filling plastic boxes with wood shavings, climbing up and down little staircases.

"Where did they all come from?" asked Victor.

"I suppose they were created here in the lab, just as I was."

"Look," said Victor, pointing down to a group off by themselves. They were quarreling, two sides arguing over one of the plastic boxes. A brown rat pushed another to the ground, cuffing him in the snout. An albino flared his claws, swiping the brown in the ear. Drops of blood spotted the white shavings. A gray rat lunged at the brown, biting down on his ankle, making him fall to the ground, where the albino mercilessly kicked him in the ribs.

Victor banged softly on the glass, trying to get their attention. They looked up at him, all with vacant stares, and went back to their business, not the least bit concerned that two rats stood outside the dome. They seemed to forget about their fight, and left the brown rat crumpled and bleeding in the shavings as though they didn't know him.

"That's not normal," said Victor. "Juveniles don't behave like that. Juniper said even Killdeer acted normal back when he was a child. It wasn't until he was nearing adulthood that he began to change."

"It's the drugs," said Billycan. "These rats don't seem to comprehend what they're doing . . . or perhaps they don't care." He thought of Topher—the wild look in his eyes, his illogical ramblings, and his unnatural strength for a rat who hadn't eaten in days.

"Duck!" barked Victor.

Walter and the female scientist, Dr. Sheppard, approached the dome. She was carrying something in a plastic cage. Their snouts just over the edge of the metal base, Billycan and Victor watched as she set the cage down and pulled a vial of black liquid from her pocket along with a syringe. "Doctor," she said, "the results are truly amazing. Not only is there a great improvement in the effects, but the time it takes for the effects to manifest themselves—it's been cut down to nothing!" Turning the vial upside down, she stuck the syringe into it and filled it with the black fluid.

"That's what I saw in the lab," said Victor.

"Doctor, would you?" she asked, nodding down at the cage.

"Oh, certainly," said Walter. Clumsily he reached into the plastic cage, nearly knocking it to the ground, and pulled out an immobile gray rat. He chuckled awkwardly. "This fellow's out cold, isn't he?"

"We feel it's far more humane this way," she said. "The rats seem to be in great pain after the injections."

"We must always look after our test subjects' welfare," said Walter.

His paws clenching into tight fists, Billycan leered across the dome. "The only welfare he's truly looked after is his own. If he had any sort of a backbone he would have tried to stop Prince years ago!" he whispered. "Instead, he's grown fat off them."

Victor suddenly grabbed Billycan's arm, frantically pulling on it. "For goodness' sake, what is it?" asked Billycan.

"That rat," Victor hissed. "I know him! He's one of the lost Hunters . . . Otto. I'm sure of it!"

"Otto," said Billycan, his mouth curling into a grimace. "That *is* him, isn't it? I recall him from the Combs. Quite an annoying fellow, if I remember correctly—though he always had his stipend at the ready, I'll give him that."

"All right, old boy," said Dr. Sheppard soothingly as Walter held the motionless Otto in his hands. "Welcome to the future." She took the needle and plunged it into Otto's belly. He didn't move at all as the black fluid entered his system. The other scientists had gathered around, all watching eagerly.

Walter held Otto up so everyone could have a look. For a few moments nothing happened, then suddenly Otto's body started shifting and writhing like a puppet attached to invisible strings. Victor cringed as Otto's bones moved beneath his skin, as though they were alive. His torso stretched and his tail pushed out from its base, growing noticeably longer. His four paws widened right before their eyes, and one by one each claw extended into a sharp, lethal point. His ears grew rounder and larger, and even his whiskers shot out a bit. Some of the scientists gasped or covered their mouths in shock.

"Wait," said Dr. Sheppard, "this is the best part."

Otto's face was changing. His snout shortened and widened. His whitish muzzle shifted back to its original youthful gray, and his aging yellow teeth instantly turned to a gleaming, healthy white.

"We have our answer, gentlemen," she said. "This miracle mineral, combined with our state-of-the-art pharmaceuticals, has produced the world's first age reversing drug. Not only will it make us look younger, in essence we will *be* younger. We can be reborn!" She looked down at Otto and then back at Walter. "And it's all thanks to Dr. Harris." The scientists cheered and shook hands, patting Walter and each other on the back.

Victor's jaw dropped in horror at the spectacle, the

realization that all the rats in the dome were once full-grown adults, now nothing more than overgrown monsters with the angelic faces of children. He wondered how many of them he might know. "They—they wouldn't do such a thing. They—they wouldn't. They couldn't!"

Billycan, not one to mince words, looked down at the rats. "They did."

"There's no way we can stop the humans," said Victor, shaking. "We are powerless against them."

"Think of those twenty dead rats, those youthful faces you just saw tossed into an incinerator. Maybe we can't stop them, maybe we'll fail quite miserably, but Victor, we have to do *something*. We have to try."

Victor's jaw stiffened. He forced himself to stop shaking. "You're right."

It was just as Silvius had predicted. The humans had found the longevity drug they'd been seeking—an undeniable fountain of youth. And what human wouldn't do just about anything for that?

CHAPTER SIXTEEN
Bats in the Belfry

JUNIPER, TAPPING HIS FOOT RESTLESSLY on the floor, listened from the vent. The breathing coming from the rats in the lab was labored and shallow. From his vantage point, nothing could be seen but the tops of cages and the muted glow coming from lab equipment. "It's been too long. Why has he not returned? Something is wrong!" he finally said.

"There's no commotion in the lab," said Vincent calmly. "If he'd been captured or something had gone awry, we'd know it. We heard the human come back. He was there only a few minutes and then left with hardly a peep."

"Vincent's right," said Cole. "If anyone was going to put up a fight, it would be Billycan. Trust me, we'd have heard it."

"Give him a little more time, Uncle," said Clover, squeezing his paw. "We have no idea how large the lab is."

Something chinked against the vent. No one moved their feet, but they raised their weapons. The sound came again, something hitting the metal and then falling back to the floor.

Juniper nodded to Carn and Suttor, who aimed their daggers at the opening. Again something was thrown, only this time it landed inside. Everyone looked down at it curiously. It was a powdery blue object in the shape of a malformed ball.

Stepping cautiously toward it, Carn nudged it with his dagger. He bent down, sniffing. "Smells ghastly," he whispered, taking a step back.

"It could be poison," said Oleander. "In the swamp, anything that's not green or brown is usually toxic."

"Like that elephant ear I ate in the swamp, that made my face swell up," said Carn. "That leaf was bright red."

"Exactly."

"Oleander!" whispered a barely audible voice from inside the lab.

Her ears perking, she looked at Carn. "Did you hear that?" Carn nodded.

"Oleander!" the muffled voice called again.

Rats began to stir in the cages below them.

Oleander got on her knees and stuck her head outside the opening of the vent, searching through the shadows. Quickly she pulled her head back inside. Her cocoa brown skin had drained of color. "It's Cobweb," she said feebly, her dark eyes wide. "How did he get here?"

Juniper and the Nightshade rescue party gathered around Cobweb and Montague. Several caged rats had spotted them entering the lab. Juniper assured those who were awake that rescue was coming, but they must stay silent for now and locked in their cages, as though nothing had changed. The rats were lean, their coats thin and drab, their eyes hollow. No one raised a fuss. Even the albinos were levelheaded, leaving Juniper to wonder where the rats who ended up insane like Topher and Liam were being caged.

"Billycan went with the scientist. He knows him from before," said Montague.

"Where did they go?" asked Vincent.

"We don't know," said Cobweb. "There was a cart . . . dead rats and bats on it. Billycan wanted to see where they were being taken. He said there could be more rats trapped somewhere else."

"Indeed," said Juniper, "this place seems endless." He looked across the lab. "Where are the bats roosting?"

"That way," said Cobweb, pointing into the dark.

"Oleander!" said Telula, skidding into the shavings on the bottom of the plastic cage. She stopped just short of the pane, a perfect landing. "So it's true! Thank the Saints, you're here!"

"Oh, Telula," said Oleander, running up to the pane, "I'm glad you're all right."

Cotton landed next to his sister. "Vincent, it's such a relief to see you. When we saw Billycan we didn't know what to think."

"Have you seen my brother?" asked Vincent.

Cotton shook his head. "No, just Billycan."

Juniper patted Vincent's shoulder. "We'll find him soon enough. He may be trapped upstairs, unable to find the lab."

Dresden came down next to Telula. The rest of the colony gathered around them or dangled from synthetic branches, listening.

"Cobweb, Montague, it's good to see you in one piece. Your efforts to save us were heroic indeed," said Dresden.

"If only we'd arrived sooner, perhaps we could have gotten you out," said Montague, staring regretfully at his brother.

"Without your valiant efforts, the swamp rats might be here as well. You got them to safety before the humans could find them. You cannot blame yourself," said Dresden. He smiled at Juniper, revealing his glossy white fangs. "Besides, our city friends have come to our assistance . . . once again."

"Let's see if we can't get you out of this fix, old friend," said Juniper, forcing a reassuring smile. He inspected the smooth plastic cage, eyeing the symmetrically placed air holes, far too small to escape from. "How have the scientists been getting bats in and out?"

Dresden gestured with his wing to the back of the cage, which was mounted to the wall. There was the outline of a door. "It opens from the other side. We've worked on the edges for days, but can't even make a dent in them."

"What's that?" asked Juniper, pointing to a plastic tube that came from the wall and into the cage.

"That's dinner," said Cotton.

"They blow insects inside the cage through the wall vent," said Telula.

"Those screws," said Vincent, pointing up to where the plastic pipe was attached to the cage by means of a square base with one screw in each corner. "They look just like the ones on the vent we came in from. If we can unscrew them, the bats can fly out through the hole, directly into the lab."

"There's nothing to hang on to," said Juniper. "We could use the air holes for grip, but they stop halfway up the cage."

A popping sound came from the wall. Everyone turned. Duncan had ripped a substantial orange cord from the electrical outlet on the wall. Immediately he followed the cord to the end attached to the machine, sat down, and began chewing at breakneck speed.

"Duncan!" said Cole, trying to keep his voice down. "What

in the name of the Saints do you think you're doing?" He remembered Duncan's growling stomach back in the museum. "You can't possibly be *that* hungry!"

"You're going to electrocute yourself," barked Suttor, staring at his brother in utter bewilderment.

"No, I'm not," said Duncan between chews. "Not if the machine's unplugged. Besides, do you have a better way to get up there?"

At first they wanted to drape the cord over the pipe, with rats holding one end of it to the floor while a single rat scaled up the other side, but the cord was simply not long enough. So instead Suttor, a former member of the Kill Army and trained in such matters, whipped the pronged end of the cord over the pipe so that it wrapped several times and anchored itself. "I never thought I'd be thankful for my Kill Army training. Life is strange." He yanked on the cord, lifting his feet off the ground and dangling for a moment, testing it with his body weight. "I don't know for how long, but it should hold long enough for me to climb up there."

"Let me go," said Cole, taking the cord from Suttor. "I don't want to risk you falling."

"I'm a trained fighter," said Suttor, puffing out his chest. "I don't need mollycoddling, you know. Mother does enough of that for both of you."

"It's not that," said Cole. "I know you are up to the task, but let your old man do the heavy lifting for once."

"Let me do it," said Oleander. "These bats are from my home." She smiled gratefully at Telula. "They are quite dear to us." A mischievous smirk spread across her face. "Besides, I'm the best climber I know."

"She's faster than most squirrels!" agreed Cotton.

"It's true," added Telula. "She nearly sprints up the cypresses back in the swamp."

Cole looked at Carn, who held his paws up as if he'd already surrendered. "Don't look at me," he said. "It's pointless! She'll do what she wants anyway."

"You're absolutely sure," said Cole. Oleander nodded. He gave the cord a finally yank, testing it one last time. "All right, then." He handed her the cord.

"Everyone, watch her closely," said Juniper. "If Oleander loses her grip, we must be ready to catch her."

Oleander wriggled up the cord until she reached the base of the plastic cage, and then used her feet for leverage against it. Everyone watched as she quickly pulled herself up to the top of the rectangular cage and then braced her feet on the plastic pipe. She straddled the pipe where it met the cage and began working on the screws, remembering how easily Billycan had loosened the ones on the vent.

She grunted, using all her strength to loosen one just a little. "C'mon, you," she whispered, "move!" She strained her forearms, and the screw finally gave way. She sighed with relief and waved down to the others, showing the freed screw in her paw. She tossed it down to them, Carn catching it before it had a chance to hit the tile floor.

"All right," said Oleander, "on to number two." She stretched out her paws and reached around to the other screw on the top of the pipe. This time she used the palm of her right paw and pulled with the left, gnashing her teeth as the screw dug into her skin. "C'mon, you wretched screw, turn!" All of a sudden the screw gave way, coming out of the cage wall and into Oleander's paws. She yelped, nearly losing her balance, but her legs held fast. She grabbed the top of the pipe with her free paw.

"Is she all right?" asked Carn, about to snatch the cord and start climbing.

"She's fine," said Clover. "See?" Oleander waved again and tossed down the screw, which Vincent caught.

"I'll believe that when she's back on solid ground," said Carn.

Oleander looked over her shoulder and down into the cage. The bats were swooping restlessly around the artificial trees, waiting for her signal. There were only two screws left on the bottom of the square plastic base holding the pipe to the cage. Rather than unscrew them, which would put her in a precarious position, having to reach down, Oleander pulled on the top part of the plastic where she'd already removed the screws. "Now then," she said, grunting as she pulled, come loose . . . please. My arms can't take much more of this." The plastic started to give way. "That's it!"

She turned back and waved down to the colony. "All right, then. Let's see how far you'll bend." She groaned as the pain in her arms increased. There was a snap as the plastic cracked off, leaving a hole large enough for a bat to escape. She shouted, "It's open! C'mon, all of you! Hurry!"

Just as her body relaxed for a moment, something hit her in the face. She grabbed for her snout, stunned by the force. She was struck again, then again, losing her grip as the hits kept coming. "Oh!" she screamed, starting to fall. She grabbed on to the edge of the hole she'd created, her legs dangling in midair.

"Oleander!" shouted Carn. "Don't let go!"

She looked up, only to be met by a flood of flying beetles pouring out from the pipe. She grimaced at the site of them, squeezing her eyes shut, their meaty black bodies flying by her head. "June bugs!" she screamed.

"Everyone, take wing!" said Dresden. "Now! Go after them before they send the entire lab into an uproar!" The bats shot out into the lab, stretching their wings, glad to be free of the tight cage, and happily tracking down the June bugs like a pack of winged bloodhounds.

"Oleander, I'm coming!" Cotton blasted out of the cage and swooped around, diving toward her. He grabbed her by the shoulders, snapping at the steady stream of beetles, who quickly veered away from his shiny teeth. He plunged to the ground, setting Oleander down lightly.

Carn grabbed her and hugged her tightly. "Are you all right?"

"I think so."

Frenzied laughter came from the other side of the lab. "Oh no," said Cotton.

"What is it?" asked Juniper.

"The beetles have awoken the Crazy Ones."

CHAPTER SEVENTEEN
The Crazy Ones

WAILING SCREECHES OF LAUGHTER SPEWED from the east section of the lab. Cages shook violently. Curses and nonsensical declarations bounced off the walls.

"The damage is done," said Juniper, running a paw over his face. "The commotion has sent them into a tailspin. Everyone, start unlocking cages." He cringed as another wail came from the east section. "And for Saints' sake, stay away from those troubled souls. They don't know the danger they're putting us in."

The rats spread out and unlocked the cages as fast as they could, climbing up and across the bars, telling the newly released rats to wait on the floor and stay away from the Crazy Ones. The bats carried the rats to cages that were in awkward positions with no easy access, making sure no creature was left behind.

It seemed all of Juniper's Hunters were dead or among the Crazy Ones. They released scores of albinos, many city rats, and nearly ten of Gwenfor's dock rats, easily recognizable by their toughened exteriors. The silver rings were missing from their ears, but the holes were still there.

Juniper had no plan. The rats gathered on the floor around him, the bats swarmed over his head, every face looking for some sort of direction. He had none to give. Billycan was missing and Victor was nowhere to be seen. Then there were the Crazy Ones—what was to happen to them? It seemed wrong to leave them to die, but releasing them would put too many at risk. He thought of Maddy, his children, the citizens of Nightshade, his Council, their sacred oath to protect all rats. He worried that for the first time he might have to break it. Covering his face for a moment, he prayed to the Saints, hoping they would guide him.

That's when he heard them . . . footsteps. Human footsteps. There was nowhere to hide, no way to get them all back into their cages, and getting them up the vent and out into the museum would take too long. Nine rats coming down was a far faster process than over a hundred rats climbing up. Suddenly inspiration struck.

"Someone's coming! Everyone, quickly now, we must scatter!" he shouted. "We must look as though we have lost our minds, as if our faculties are completely gone. Act wild—out of control. Make them think we're sick and dying. Dresden, your colony must crowd around their heads, flap your wings, graze their skin. Rats, we must frighten the humans as only rats can! Show your teeth, flare your claws—but above all, no violence! It will only cause them to take arms against us. We must make whoever's coming leave the lab. It's our only chance of getting out of here alive!"

Juniper's hackles rose as he heard the door opening. "Not yet! Wait for my signal!"

Walter entered the darkened lab with Dr. Sheppard. She groaned and shook her head. "They're at it again," she said. "At this late hour you'd think even our little Crazy Ones would need rest. Don't you think it's time to put them to sleep, Dr. Harris?" She gave a pained smile. "I know you care for them, but it's the humane thing to do. Like you said in the Clean Room, if we don't look out for their welfare, no one will."

"Charlotte, using my own words against me," said Walter, chuckling. "Very clever. It's late. Why don't we discuss it in the morning?" His face shifted to a serious expression. "I must say, I'm exhausted. Sometimes I think I could sleep for days."

"But Doctor, you've finally discovered what you've been searching for all these years. You're going to be famous! Your findings are going to change the course of history—*forever.*"

"I've no need for fame, Charlotte. And those findings come at a price."

"Yes, sir," she replied. A rat screeched from the other side of the lab. She rolled her eyes. "I better attend to our little friends. I have just the thing to calm them down." She hit the light switches and row upon row of light panels flickered on. She looked around and gasped. "Doctor! The cages—they're empty!"

"Now!" shouted Juniper.

The bats got to them first. Dr. Sheppard had removed her protective headgear when she left the Clean Room. "Go for her hair!" shouted Telula to the colony. "Humans can't stand it—drives them mad, especially the females!"

The bats circled around Dr. Sheppard's head, grabbing locks of her dark hair, pulling and tugging on it, pretending to get tangled in it. She screamed, covering her face and jumping up and down as rats pulled and clawed at her shoes and pant legs. "Doctor, what's happening?" she cried. "They've all gone mad!"

Walter was in no position to answer her. Rats jumped from rows of cages. Landing on his back, they pulled on his ears and yanked his white, fluffy hair. At least twenty rats had crawled atop his workstation, knocking whatever they could to the ground. Monitors crashed to the floor in a smoking heap. Vials and beakers shattered into tiny pieces. Pens flew at him like spears, bouncing off his lab coat. "No! Don't do that!" he shouted as rats ripped apart his papers and hurled them into the air, sending them raining down in a tornado of white.

"What did you give them?" he demanded.

"Nothing, Doctor, I swear!" said Dr. Sheppard, desperately trying to protect her eyes as wings unfurled in her face.

Walter's eyes widened as a group of dock rats grabbed their throats, pretending to choke. They threw their bodies to the ground, coughing and gagging, writhing as if in pain. Bats plunged from the ceiling, landing on the floor and tables in awkward heaps, screeching with feigned agony. "Bless the Saints!" Walter yelled. "They're all dying!"

"That's it!" shouted Juniper over the clamor. "Keep at it! It's working!"

"Victor!" yelled Vincent. He pushed through the stumbling rats and leaped over squirming bats, racing toward the door the scientists had come through.

Baffled, Billycan and Victor stood and watched, completely dumbfounded by the unfolding mayhem.

Vincent grabbed Victor by the shoulders, shaking him. "You're alive!" He hugged him firmly and then shook him again. "Don't ever pull something like that again, do you understand me? You had us all worried sick!"

"I'm sorry," said Victor, flinching as another beaker crashed to the floor. "The dead bodies in the morgue, I just couldn't bear it. Things like that aren't supposed to happen in Nightshade."

"It's all right," said Vincent, barely dodging a metal test-tube rack as it came barreling toward him.

"What happened to your leg?" asked Victor, eyeing the deep wound.

"I'll tell you later," said Vincent, blocking an oncoming test tube with his elbow. "This isn't exactly the best time to explain."

"This is the worst display of bad theater I've ever encountered," said Billycan, stepping over a convulsing rat. "Whose bright idea was this?"

"Mine," said Juniper. "We had no choice." He nodded at Walter. "Besides, the humans are buying it."

"Humans are more foolish than I thought," said Billycan.

Flailing his arms and tripping over fallen equipment, Walter tried to keep the bats at bay as they swatted him in the head with their wings and pulled at his ears with their claws. The rats crawled up his trouser legs and hung from the bottom of his lab coat.

Dr. Sheppard was sobbing, covering her head with her lab coat, shivering under a desk. "Why are they sick, Doctor?" She blew her nose in her sleeve. "All our research—it's ruined!"

"Everyone, it's time to die!" shouted Juniper. "Make it big!" The rats hollered and moaned, clutching their throats and bellies as they dropped where the stood, kicking their feet, their eyelids fluttering, their tongues lolling. The bats flew in crooked circles, hurling themselves into the air, dropping to the floor, their bodies jerking and flopping as if they had no control.

"Where did you go?" asked Juniper as he and Billycan fell to the floor with the others.

"Victor can tell you later," Billycan replied. "Listen to me, brother, closely. Get these rats out of here, up the vent and out the sewer, just the way we came in. The bats are in far better health than the rats right now. They can carry anyone who can't climb up the vent. Understand?"

"Even with the bats, that will take too long. The scientists will be able to stop us."

"I will buy you time," said Billycan.

"What are you planning?"

"I don't know. . . ."

"Everyone, now!" Juniper called out. "It's time to meet your makers!"

One by one, the rats and bats stopped moving and fell silent. All exhausted from their feverish performance, it was not hard for them to lie motionless. Other than a random shout from the Crazy Ones, the lab fell perfectly still . . . almost peaceful.

"Charlotte?" said Walter, finally opening his eyes. He spotted her under the desk, shaking hysterically. "It's over now. Look, they're all . . . dead." He stepped lightly, avoiding the animals, and held out a hand to her, pulling her to her feet. "Are you all right?"

"I—I think so." She sniffled, wiping her eyes. She put a hand to her heart, her eyes taking in all her months of research, now dead and lifeless on the tiles. "What happened to them, Dr. Harris? What killed them?"

"I have no idea," he said limply.

Dr. Sheppard looked at the rows of open cages. "Doctor, what if those activists—what if they did this? I know the lab's been kept a secret, but what if someone leaked our location? That would explain all the animals free in the lab." She crouched down, staring at a pile of motionless rats. "They certainly didn't unlock the cages themselves." She suddenly gasped. "What if the activists poisoned them?"

"But that makes no sense. Why would animal rights activists kill the very thing they're fighting to protect?"

"Then the government!" she said. "They've always been after Prince." Her face hardened. "Maybe they're scared of what our discoveries might bring to the world, or infuriated that they didn't get to it first."

Shaking his head, Walter straightened out his lab coat and smoothed back his hair. His face was pale and devoid of emotion, his eyes wandering over the chaotic lab. "Charlotte, who do you think has been funding this project? People—important people with power—will be the first to double their lifespans, regain their youth, perhaps even live forever. Who do you think would have the most to gain from that?"

"You mean the government is—"

Walter held up his hand, silencing her. "Charlotte, none of that matters now."

"But don't you want me to call someone? Shouldn't we call the police, or at least contact someone at Prince?"

"No," he said flatly. "Police are not necessary . . . and I will deal with Prince myself." He stepped over a pile of rats and picked up his broken spectacles from the floor. He studied them while he spoke. "I trust that as usual you're the last person here."

"Yes, Doctor." Her eyes scanned the lab longingly.

He finally looked at her. "Charlotte, I need you to document this. We need to ensure this drug never comes to fruition . . . not after what we've witnessed."

"We could start again, though," said Dr. Sheppard. "Maybe this time—"

"No," said Walter, cutting her off. "This drug has been my life's work, and it's caused nothing but pain and suffering. It all started with Serena. Even back then we were trying to harness the power of that volcano . . . and look where that got us. Many people suffered, not just our test subjects."

Dr. Sheppard swallowed hard. "You're right, Doctor." She looked up at the open cages and then down at the floor. The camcorder was smashed to pieces, lying next to a group of crumpled bats.

Walter followed her gaze. He took a phone from his lab coat and handed it to her. "Use mine. Prince gave it to me . . . high-tech imagery." He nodded at the camcorder. "Better than that old thing."

Holding back her tears, she took the phone and began recording the scene.

"I think I got it all," said Dr. Sheppard. "This should be powerful footage."

"And that's exactly what we're looking for," said Walter, "something that will make the executives understand they must stop this madness."

A Crazy One screeched from the back row of cages. "What do you make of the other rats, though?" asked Dr. Sheppard. "How do you think they're still alive?"

"That's simple," Walter replied. "They went mad. We stopped giving them the drug."

"Oh . . . of course," said Dr. Sheppard, shaking her head. "I'm not thinking straight."

"Nor should you be, not after what you've seen tonight. You are a brilliant scientist and I consider you a friend, but Charlotte, I think it's time you moved on. Clearly there's nothing here for you now." He forced a smile. "Consider yourself laid off."

She swallowed again and gathered her things. She held out the phone to Walter. "Your phone, Doctor."

"No, I need you to keep it. Give a copy of the footage to every news team in town. This is your chance to do the right thing, to save lives. We're both doctors, Charlotte. We both took an oath which we swore to fulfill to the best of our ability and judgment. We swore to do no harm, and that means stopping others from doing it as well. This footage will help ensure that." He looked at her intently and then down at the dead animals.

Nodding, Dr. Sheppard put the phone in her pocket. She headed for the door, turning back just before she opened it. "Doctor, what are you going to do now? As you said, this was your life's work."

"I told you earlier, our findings come at a price. It's high time I paid it."

Walter milled around the lab, agitated and edgy. Stepping over dead creatures, he wrung his hands. He headed for the door, but quickly turned back. He began picking up all his fallen papers, clutching them haphazardly in his arms.

"Juniper," whispered Billycan as they lay still, "your satchel. I need it."

"What for?"

"Please, just give it to me."

"Very well," Juniper replied. He eyed Walter, who was racing hastily about the lab, snatching up papers near the bat cage. Juniper rolled over, grabbed his satchel, and slid it over to Billycan, who concealed it under his stomach. "What do you want my satchel for?"

"I don't want your blasted satchel," said Billycan with a wily grin. "I just happen to need it. Infernal thing has only been a nuisance to me. Cost me the High Ministry, to be sure."

"I hope you're joking," said Juniper, raising an eyebrow.

"Must I remind you who saved your grizzled old hide from Hecate?"

Juniper chuckled softly. "*You* did, brother."

"Now, then," said Billycan, "you must get all these tragically departed creatures—along with their unfortunate acting skills—out of here. The minute he leaves, you lead the charge. If anyone can organize rats to get somewhere they're not supposed to be, it's you. You can save them."

"But what about you?"

"What about me?" asked Billycan. "If you hadn't noticed, I can take care of myself."

"I can't just leave you here. You saved all of us from Killdeer's sisters. You saved Nightshade from Hecate. Billycan, it's *my* turn now . . . to save you."

Billycan looked at all the rats and bats strewn around him, remembering every crime he'd ever committed. The pain and guilt would always remain. He reached for Juniper's paw and grasped it in his own. "You save all of them, you save me."

Walter seemed to be done collecting his papers. He was headed toward the door.

"Now then, get them out of here," said Billycan. "I can't stand to look at their limp bodies any longer." He eyed a plump bat sprawled out a few inches from him. "You know how I like bat."

"I'm not going to see you again, am I?"

"Stranger things have happened, haven't they?" Billycan touched the raised black scar that traveled across his snout. "You and I are not carving each other's eyes out or ripping apart each other's snouts, for one thing."

"I couldn't hurt you now any more than I could hurt Julius or Nomi. We're family. You are my brother."

"That I am."

Juniper and Billycan lay still as Walter made his way to the door. As soon as Walter's white lab coat disappeared into the dark, Billycan bolted to his feet. "Another time, then, brother." With a devilish smirk he winked at Juniper, climbed swiftly up a row of cages, whipped around a corner, and was gone.

CHAPTER EIGHTEEN
The End

WALTER DIDN'T RUN, but walked at a determined pace. Whatever doubt or confusion he had felt in the lab seemed to have melted away. He'd taken all his scientific papers, all the documents that could help Prince start up its research again, down to the incinerator and burned them to ashes.

As the elevator climbed, he looked down at the metal cart he was returning with. He wondered how many victims of his research had lain on it, all cold and stiff. This would be the last time he'd ever have to use it, and for that he was relieved.

Animals didn't have souls. As a doctor, a man of science, that was something he was taught to believe, something he would swear to around others, but in truth he never believed it. How could he? The rats he worked with over the years were too smart, too clever, to not have some sort of spirit within them. Every time more of his research subjects died, so did a piece of him . . . the piece of him that wanted to believe, the piece of him that knew what he was doing was very, very wrong.

He was glad it was finally over.

He pushed the cart out of the elevator and back to the darkened lab. He unlocked the door and hit the switches. The light panels flickered on, causing a few of the Crazy Ones to stir in their cages.

Walter's mouth fell open. He dropped the key card from his trembling hand and froze in his tracks.

All the creatures that had lain dead on the floor mere moments ago had vanished.

Amid the broken equipment and smashed vials and beakers, Walter wiped off his seat with a cloth, sending shards of glass to the floor. He sat down and took in the scene. Where did all the dead creatures go? Who took them? They didn't just get up and walk away.

He exhaled heavily, glancing at the row of empty cages next to his desk. He looked at the one that had held the two gray rats he'd taken a shine to. They'd sat right next to him every day as he toiled through his research.

The hairs on Walter's neck suddenly stood on end. There was a rat in the cage. It was in shadow, but Walter could see it moving in the back.

He tilted his head, trying to catch a glimpse of it. "Hey there, fella. It's okay, you can come out."

Juniper's satchel strapped over his chest, Billycan walked slowly to the front of the cage, on two feet, something he'd never done in front of a human. He pushed open the metal door and stepped out. He stood before Walter.

Instinctively Walter pulled back from the rat. He was

expecting one of the two grays. This was an albino, a rather large one, standing on two feet, no less. Was this creature senseless like the rats on the other side of the wall, just waiting to attack him? The rat didn't move. Unlike the sickly rats, its eyes did not wander aimlessly. Its body did not twitch or spasm. It looked quite thoughtful actually, staring at him.

He leaned in cautiously, trying to get a better look. "You've been through a lot, haven't you?" he said in a soothing tone, noticing the thick black scar running down the rat's snout. "I bet you've got some stories to tell." Just then Walter noticed the rat had something strapped to it, something brown and leathery. "What have you got there, fella?"

Billycan opened Juniper's satchel and reached inside. He felt around for a moment until he found what he was looking for. Carefully he took a step forward and placed the silver disk in front of Walter.

Confounded by the vision of the gift-bearing rat before him, Walter covered his mouth and stared at Billycan, thunderstruck. Billycan took another step closer and pushed the silver disk toward Walter with his foot.

Walter looked at Billycan and then down at the object. Gingerly he picked up the silver disk and held it in his palm. He looked down at it and read the number, and then his eyes darted back to Billycan. "It's . . . it's not possible," he whispered. His voice was taut and dry. "But I thought you'd died in the fire . . . or were exterminated afterward . . . Billy?"

Billycan smiled. He didn't know how a rat smile looked to a human, but he didn't care. Walter knew who he was. He remembered him.

"Bless the Saints," said Walter. Tears welled in his eyes. "I knew—or at least I thought I knew—that there was much more to you rats than met the eye, but how could I be sure?" He smiled feebly. "Billy-*can*... remember that? Because I thought you could do anything. You were special. I wonder, are the other rats as clever as you?" Billycan nodded. Walter laughed out loud. "You just nodded at me." He took in a jagged breath, and then let it out. "You understand me! This is remarkable. I never—" His words suddenly halted. He looked at the destruction around him and then back at Billycan. "You ... you tricked us, didn't you—all of you?" He ran a hand over his face and laughed again. "None of you were dead. You escaped! Humans bamboozled by animals!" He got down very close to Billycan and looked into his eyes. "You are as smart as us, aren't you, Billycan?"

Walter's eyes swelled with sudden fear. He put a nervous hand over his heart. "Prince—they can never find out about you! No one can ever find out, do you understand? They'll do whatever they can to find out your secrets, and boy, do you have secrets!" He laughed again. "More secrets than anyone could ever imagine!"

Billycan glanced around the table looking for something. He shook his head, unable to find it. He looked at Walter's pocket and pointed.

"What is it, boy? What are you looking at?" Walter felt the front pocket of his lab coat. The only thing in it was a pen. Billycan jumped up and down. "Oh, my pen? You want it?" Billycan nodded.

He took the pen from Walter and retrieved a crumpled piece of paper stuck between the row of cages and the edge of the table. Getting down on his haunches and knees, he spread out the paper, took the pen, and began to write.

"Bless the Saints," said Walter, mystified. "You can write."

Standing back up, Billycan handed the paper to Walter. It had one letter and one number on it: C-4.

Billycan had remembered seeing the packages down by the volcano where the men were digging. He'd seen the same letter and number months before in the hot Toscan jungle. Bandits had been blasting away at an old mine, hoping to find precious stones still trapped inside. Nothing came of it, except a great deal of noise and destruction and one dimwitted man losing his arm in the blast. "C-4" was what was written on the crates they had with them.

After reading it, Walter exhaled a shaky breath. "You mean the volcano, don't you? You want to get rid of it, once and for all. You want me to help you."

Billycan nodded.

Carrying Billycan in the crook of his arm, Walter walked toward a substantial metal cabinet on the edge of the circular walkway surrounding the crater. He unlocked it with a gold key. Inside the cabinet there was nothing but a small screen and keypad, which lit up a brilliant red as the doors swung open. He began punching in a long series of numbers on the keypad. He then set his hand on the screen, and the color shifted from red to green. With a resounding snap the screen and keypad fell away, vanishing into some secret chamber within the cabinet.

Walter set Billycan down inside the cabinet. He retrieved another phone from his back pocket, his personal phone. He pressed a button and waited a moment. A faint voice came from it. "No, I'm not on my way," he said. "Yes, I know it's late." He hesitated before he spoke again. "What we've always talked about . . . it's happening. Abigail, we always knew this was a possibility. My research papers—destroy them. Prince must never get its hands on them. Yes, the safe in the closet." Sobs came from the phone. "Please, you must keep your head." He wiped his eyes. "I'll be fine. It's finally over. Call the children and get everyone to our secret place; that way no one from Prince will bother you about this. It's all paid for, just go. I promise . . . I'll be there soon. Abigail, I have to go now." He put a hand on his forehead, covering his eyes. "I love you too. Yes, I'll be careful. See you shortly."

The cabinet was filled with packages, each one wrapped neatly in brown paper, each no larger than a box of butter. Billycan read the black writing on the brown paper. There was a "C" and a "4" in block lettering.

Walter shoved the phone back into his pocket and quickly began removing packages from the cabinet, placing them in a wheelbarrow. Billycan helped as much he could, handing more packages to Walter each time he returned.

As soon as the barrow was filled, Walter rolled it over to the formation and began placing the packages all around the base of the massive rock. Billycan used Juniper's satchel to drag more packages toward Walter, who spoke to him as he frantically readied the explosives. "I should have stopped them years ago, but I was too afraid. Anyone who spoke out against

Prince . . . their careers were ruined or they seemed to disappear. I couldn't let that happen, but even back then, I knew what they were doing—what we were doing—was wrong." He looked at Billycan's snout. "But look at you—you're a fighter, I can tell. You're strong, a survivor. You're not like me, Billycan. You're better." He positioned the last block of C-4. "There. I think we're done."

After he'd placed the last package, Walter went back to the cabinet, returning with an armful of wires, a box cutter, tape, and other miscellaneous items that Billycan could not identify. Working furiously. Walter laced the wires and explosives together. "We must make sure the blasting caps are in place and not a single wire comes loose."

Groaning as he straightened up, Walter got to his feet, which somehow felt lighter than before. "We've got to get you out of here," he said to Billycan. "I've watched an army of rats die in my time . . . by my own hand, I'm sorry to say. I don't want you to be the next . . . especially you." He held out his hands to him. "C'mon, boy, I'll get you somewhere safe. I'm sure you have a home somewhere."

The truth was that the Catacombs, the swamp, Tosca, none of them would ever be Billycan's home. Nightshade City held those he loved, but it, too, would never be home. It was his son's home, and that was good enough. If Billycan *did* have a home, it was the lab. After all these years it was what he knew best. He looked around the cave, saying good-bye to whatever lay in that volcano that had made him who he was.

Billycan looked at Walter one last time and ran off into the dark.

Dawn was coming. The bats had quickly departed, making the long journey back to the swamp to find a new home where

Topsiders could never find them, away from the chapel. The dock rats had left for the shores of the Hellgate, already plotting their revenge on the humans. The city rats raced back to their attics, basements, and alleyways.

All that remained were Cobweb and Montague, the Council, a few rats who didn't know how to find their way home, and the albinos—those who had never had a home outside the lab's sterile white walls. They gathered in the park. "My mother was a lab rat for a time," Juniper told them. "Her other son, my brother, is an albino just like you. He was born in a lab, same as you all, but the difference is, he didn't know he had a family—you do. Nightshade City is made up of rats who have fought to stay together. Even through great loss and death, we have remained a family, not always by blood but a family by love for our fellow rat. What I'm saying is, you are welcome. You can stay a single night or until your dying day. The choice is yours."

Before anyone could consider, a deafening blast pierced the air, an eruption so furious the ground shook under their feet. Every head turned to see a colossal ball of fire shoot skyward, dark plumes of smoke and debris following after it. Glass shattered and car alarms went off. Shouts and screams came from citizens as they looked out into the smoking gloom.

Clover took Vincent's paw. "The museum! Look!"

"Bless the Saints," said Juniper, grabbing Victor's shoulder, his legs weakening at the sight. "Billycan!"

"After our mock attack, that look in Billycan's eyes," said Cole. "You knew he was up to something."

"But what about the other rats?" said Carn. "The ones that didn't get out . . . the Crazy Ones?"

"They're surely dead," said Juniper. "May their souls rest with the Saints." He bowed his head, thinking about Topher and

Liam. "I can't say I'm sorry about that. No rat—no creature—should ever have to live like that."

"What about Billycan?" asked Clover. "Do you think he got out in time?"

"I'm beginning to think he's capable of escaping just about anything," Juniper replied weakly. "Never have I known a rat who can disappear so quickly, and materialize when you least expect it." His shoulders slumped. "I hope he got out alive...." He thought of Lenore, their mother. Somehow he pictured her and Billycan together, but he didn't want that, not yet. He needed more time. His voice dropped to an inaudible whisper. "Please, Saints ... see him through. Please."

"Do you think we'll see him again?"

Juniper didn't answer. He stared blankly at the fire rising from the museum.

CHAPTER NINETEEN
Gifts

IT HAD BEEN THREE MONTHS since the explosion at the museum. Blaming it on the ancient sewer system, its water eroding the earth under the museum, city officials proclaimed the explosion to be the result of a sinkhole, the sheer impact of it causing anything combustible in the museum to explode.

What was left of the museum was to be permanently sealed off. The city health inspectors were worried an unknown substance—the curious black dust that coated the blast site and debris—might cause lung damage, cancer, even birth deformities. The government had barricaded the area, armed forces guarding it day and night from nosy onlookers and tourists who wanted to get a look at the sunken museum before it was lost to the world forever.

One death had been reported by the Trillium news stations. A scientist, Dr. Walter Lee Harris, had died in the explosion. No one knew what he was doing on museum property at such an early hour. Authorities reported that he might have been out for an early morning stroll. His family, who had recently departed the country, were unavailable for comment, their whereabouts unknown. There was no mention of Prince Pharmaceuticals.

"Well?" said Clover, looking at her uncle in the mirror's reflection. "What do you think?"

"Why, you're just . . . *you*. You've no sash, no ribbons or bows, no jewels around your neck or flowers behind your ears." He sighed with satisfaction. "You're simply perfect."

"I must say," said Mother Gallo, joining her husband, "you are quite lovely. Besides, you never were one for my ribbons and bows." She laughed. "I suppose I will just have to find a way to live with that." Nomi pulled at her tail. Mother Gallo swooped her up in her arms and twirled her in a circle. "But I have you, little one. You love my ribbons and bows!" Nomi giggled. "C'mon, you, let's go find your brothers." Mother Gallo patted Clover's shoulder. "Not too long, now, dear. Everyone's waiting."

The room seemed very quiet after Mother Gallo and Nomi left. Juniper wasn't his normal jovial self. He hadn't been in some time. He sat vacantly in Council meetings or sat stoically by the fire. He'd finally accepted Billycan's death, but the pain was still there. Clover looked at him thoughtfully. "You're thinking about him again, aren't you? You miss him."

"Such a clever niece you are," he said, sitting down at the table. "You can always read me like a book. I think he would have enjoyed today. You are his niece, too, after all."

"Uncle Billycan," said Clover. "I do like the sound of it."

Juniper smiled. "Truth be told, I miss him terribly. I feel there was so much about him I'll never know, and that he never lived the life he was meant to."

Clover looked at Trilok's medal, resting on Juniper's chest.

"There's been so much death surrounding that medal, don't you think?"

"Yes," said Juniper, nodding, "Billycan's included, but also so much happiness. When Trilok formed the Catacombs and was given this medal, it was done out of gratitude. So many rats were truly thankful for what he'd done. He'd given them a home, a place where they'd feel safe. And when we defeated Killdeer, when the citizens were freed from that nightmare, this medal was a symbol of that—of freedom. The death that looms around this medal is a reminder of our past, tragedy turning to triumph, something we all should revel in."

"And Vincent wonders where I get my sunny outlook, as he likes to call it," said Clover. "Clearly it runs in the family."

There was a knock at the door. "Juniper, are you in there?"

"Yes, Carn, please come in."

Carn and Oleander entered the Belancort quarters. In Carn's paws was a small burlap sack. "We have something for you." He set it on the table. "It's from Tosca."

"Tosca?"

"Yes," said Oleander. "We went to the alley of the Brimstone Building, to check in with Dresden's colony, and Cotton and Telula had brought this."

"How did they get this all the way from Tosca?"

"The Canyon Bats, who dwell in Tosca," said Oleander, "are friends of the Toscan rats."

"Billycan mentioned something about that. The Toscan rats' leader, Silvius—he was instrumental in forming that alliance."

Carn and Oleander swapped glances. "Yes ... about Silvius," said Carn. "He passed away recently, in his sleep."

"That's unfortunate," said Juniper. "He was a rat I someday wanted to meet." He looked at the sack. "So what is this?"

"Something you need to see," said Carn.

Raising an eyebrow quizzically, Juniper opened the sack. Instantly, by touch, he knew what was inside. He pulled out the silver tag. "Another lab tag? Did this belong to Silvius?"

"Yes . . . but you must look at it," pressed Carn, "please."

Juniper's heart tightened in his chest as he regarded the etched metal. The front of the tag was engraved, number 111 and the word "Father." The back of the tag read "Prince Laboratories" and the date "October 31." "It all matches," he said in a whisper. "Billycan's, Silvius's, our mother's tag, they are all connected, all the same." He rested a paw over Trilok's medal. "Silvius . . . he was Billycan's father. All that time, he was in Tosca with his father . . . and he never knew." Juniper's wounded expression slowly shifted into a grin. "He'd been searching for family, and he found it." Juniper chuckled. His chuckle turned into a laugh, a laugh so loud that Carn, Oleander, and Clover shifted awkwardly, concerned for him. "He *found* it!"

"Found what?" asked Carn. "This is a sad moment and you're acting like it's a celebration."

"My boy, it *is* a celebration!" Juniper bolted up from his chair. He plucked Clover off her feet and swung her around in a circle.

"Uncle, what's got into you?" she asked as he set her on her feet. "Are you all right?"

"Never better, my dear. Never better! Don't you see? Billycan found his *family* after all this time." He looked up at the ceiling, a smile upon his face. "Take care of them, Saints. Lenore, Silvius, Billycan . . . finally together." He straightened out his cloak, grinning at the youthful faces before him. "I think it's high time we finally had a wedding, don't you?"

"I . . . wish it," Clover said, looking around the Council Chamber anxiously, slightly gun-shy considering the last time she'd been about to say those words. No axes or arrows this time, only the smiling faces of those she knew and loved.

The official nodded at the guests and then back at Clover and Vincent. He took both their paws in his and then placed Vincent's over Clover's. He cleared his throat. "And so, in front of these witnesses, let the couple confirm their bond." His cracked lips finally formed a smile. He eyed Vincent, raising his brow. "Well, son, what are you waiting for?"

With everyone staring, Vincent's cheeks grew hot and he felt dizzy.

An irked voice broke the awkward silence. "For Saints' sake, will you go on and kiss her already? My whiskers will be gray before you finally make your move!" Everyone tried not to laugh, but it couldn't be helped. Juniper and the older males snickered under their breath, while Carn and Suttor nearly fell off their chairs, even with Oleander's scolding. After all, they were all thinking the same thing, but Victor was the only one with the nerve to say it.

Vincent glared at his brother. He turned back to Clover, but it was too late, she was already moving in for the kiss, catching him just as he turned his head. He nearly lost his footing for a second, but once his feet steadied he was fine—very fine, indeed.

"Ick! They're kissing," whispered Julius, disgusted. He squirmed in his chair and made a sour face.

Victor nudged him. "Just wait a few years, little rat. Won't be so appalling then, you'll see."

"He's right, Julius," whispered Texi, smiling coyly at Ulrich. "You find the right one, it'll be wonderful."

"Take your time, though," said Ulrich. "Sometimes it takes a while." He squeezed Texi's paw. "But when you find her, you'll know it."

The official spoke, his scratchy voice carrying throughout the chamber. "And as they wished, so it is done!"

Everyone got to their feet, clapping and cheering. Juniper kissed Clover on the cheek as they stepped off the makeshift platform. He embraced Vincent and whispered in his ear. "Welcome to the family, son . . . officially, that is. You've always been part of it." He glanced around the room, making sure he saw everyone. His wife and children, his Council and their families—then something occurred to him. Something he'd spoken with Cole about, but never mentioned to anyone else. He patted Trilok's medal, thinking it would be for the very last time. Vincent had come a long way since he was a lost young rat making his way down to Nightshade that first time, his frightened brother in tow. He was grown. He was smart. He knew who he was, and he lived his life guided by the bright spirit of his father, Julius Nightshade.

It was time.

CHAPTER TWENTY
Reborn

HE WOKE UP UNDER A PILE OF DEBRIS, sprawled on the ground, surrounded by broken furniture, shattered glass, plumbing fixtures, and mounds of black dust. He didn't know how long he'd been there; it felt like mere days, but given the thick layer of dust coating him, he reasoned it had to be far longer. He pulled himself up and stretched out his body, which felt remarkably flexible given the crooked position he'd woken up in. He tried to remember exactly how he'd gotten to this place. Though his mind was alert, his memories were vague; in fact, he wasn't sure if they were memories at all . . . perhaps he had been dreaming.

He threaded his way through the wreckage. It was dark, but his vision was quite clear, as though the world had suddenly become illuminated. He came across a shattered mirror, still in its gilded frame. After brushing away as much dust as he could from his fur, he made a fist and wiped away a clean circle on the mirror. He regarded his reflection. He was young—not a tot, mind you, not even a child, but young—a rat who looked to be just coming into his own. He thought he'd be older. He bared his teeth; they were impeccably white and razor sharp, his gums fresh and pink. His jaw was thick and his muzzle long, giving him a rather noble air. His snout—it didn't look right to him, not at all. Frankly, it looked too perfect. He recalled it differently, terribly flawed somehow. He glanced down at his body. No clear image would register in his head, but he thought of old wounds and battle scars. To his surprise, his long arms and legs were free of scars and bruises, his torso rigid, lean, and muscular, and his thick coat remarkably shiny, in spite of the never-ending dust that fell from it. His eyes struck him the most. They were a dark red, nearly plum. He liked them. They looked kind.

As he stared at his reflection, two rats materialized behind them. One was long and tall, with a clean, lustrous white coat. The rat smiled confidently, a stately appearance about him, but he looked nice, the kind of rat who'd help someone he barely knew, an honorable rat. The other rat was slight, with thick, shimmering fur the color of raisins, and buttery-yellow eyes that flickered boldly. She was quite pretty. She reminded him of someone, but he wasn't sure who. He smiled at the two older rats behind him, hoping they'd follow him out of this place.

His memory was a miasma of faces and things. He still had no idea how he got there, or really anything about himself. The more he thought about it, the more things faded away like dreams do. He knew one thing, though; he was going to get out of this dank, dirty hole. He yearned to see the sunlight. He would miss the black dust, though. He liked the smell of it. The scent reminded him of something, made him feel connected to it, but of course he couldn't say what that something was.

Making his way up the tall mountain of wreckage, he

came across a long wooden sign. In ornate gold letters it read THE LORDS OF TRILLIUM. He scratched his head. A lord, someone important, someone who had a great deal of power, but he had no interest in that. The long sign did make for good climbing, though, allowing him easy access to the city street. Daylight was just peeking over the horizon. He peered over his shoulder, making sure the other two rats had kept up with him.

There were large men with guns guarding the hole, their backs to him. He wondered why a hole full of useless, broken things would be so important to anyone that they'd guard it with guns. As he walked behind them, he heard one say the hole would be sealed off permanently today. He turned and looked down into it, still wondering how he got there. For some reason he didn't think his memory of it would ever return. Oddly, he was at ease with that. The male rat rested a warm paw on his shoulder. He knew it was time to go.

It rained lightly, rinsing the black dust out of his white coat. He liked the feel of the water on his skin, light washing away the darkness. He smiled at the other two rats as the three of them walked past the barricades. He thought about names and places. What would he call himself? Where would he go? A feeling of freedom came over him. His future, wherever it led, was entirely up to him.

The female rat took his paw and smiled. The male smiled as well, putting a snow-white arm around his shoulder. Their names—he felt like they were coming back to him.

He pointed at the sun rising higher and higher in the sky. "Let's go there," he told his companions, "wherever it leads." They nodded in agreement.

He looked back one final time, glancing at the tattered brown satchel he dragged behind him.